Ballet Stars

Dear Reader,

Ballet has always been a very important part of my life, something I've shared with friends and practised just for myself. It's the first thing I want to do when I feel great, and something that always makes me feel better if I'm having a bad day. Learning new steps is fun, and practising a dance until you get it right can give you a big sense of achievement. And performing for an audience is the greatest feeling in the world!

I hope you'll enjoy reading about the dancing adventures that Tash and her friends have in Ballet Stars, and that the stories might inspire you to get up and dance yourself. I know, if you do, you'll have loads of fun.

Lots of love,

Jane Lawes

PS Tash and her friends get to dance en pointe because they have proper training and the right shoes. But you must never try to do that without a ballet teacher! Without training, you could get hurt.

For all my dancing friends, past and present

First published in 2015 by Usborne Publishing Ltd.,
Usborne House, 83-85 Saffron Hill, London EC1N 8RT, England.
www.usborne.com

Copyright © Jane Lawes, 2015

The right of Jane Lawes to be identified as the author
of this work has been asserted by her in accordance with the
Copyright, Designs and Patents Act, 1988.

Cover: illustration of dancers by Barbara Bongini;
pattern of flowers © Nataliia Kucherenko/Shutterstock

The name Usborne and the devices ♀ ⊕ are Trade Marks of
Usborne Publishing Ltd.

This is a work of fiction. The characters, incidents, and dialogues are products of the
author's imagination and are not to be construed as real. Any resemblance to actual
events or persons, living or dead, is entirely coincidental.

A CIP catalogue record for this book is available from the British Library.

JFMAM JASOND/15   ISBN 9781409583554   03461/1

Printed in the UK.

Usborne
Ballet
Stars

Sparkling
Solo

Jane Lawes

USBORNE

Chapter 1

Tash closed her eyes, just for a moment, and let the book she was reading fall shut in her lap. The April sunshine was warm and comforting on her face. It was the first Saturday afternoon that had been sunny enough for the students at Aurora House Ballet School to take their homework outside onto the grass.

"Keep your head still," ordered Dani, one of Tash's two best friends.

Dani was sitting behind her, plaiting Tash's long, dark brown hair.

"Sorry." Tash smiled at Dani over her shoulder, then opened *Goodnight Mister Tom* again, the book she was reading for their English class.

They had exams in all their academic classes this term, and Tash knew that she needed to do well. She'd been given a full scholarship to the school because she'd shown exceptional potential as a ballet dancer at her audition, and she intended to work hard to keep it. After all, Mum couldn't afford to pay for her to stay at Aurora House without it.

Dani finished one plait and moved to the other side of Tash's head to do the rest. Anisha, their other best friend, was lying on her stomach in front of Tash with her maths textbook and exercise book spread open on the grass. She was holding a pen in her hand, but Tash hadn't seen her write anything for at least ten minutes. Right now, she had her chin down on her folded arms and it was very possible that she was asleep.

"It feels so much nicer with my hair off my back," Tash said, when Dani finished the second plait.

"Having long hair is so uncomfortable when it's hot," Dani agreed. Her own light-blonde hair was pulled up into a messy bun.

"The problems of being a ballerina in training!" laughed Tash.

Aurora House was strict on many things, including keeping your uniform neat and tidy, being on time for meals and lessons, no nail varnish on weekdays, and hair. No one was allowed to cut their hair too short to go up into the perfect ballet bun they had to wear from Monday to Friday. Tash didn't mind it, but Dani got really annoyed with hers getting in the way when it was down, and Tash had no idea how Anisha, whose hair was longer than anyone else's, could stand it in the summer.

"Shall we wake her up?" Dani asked, pointing at Anisha.

Tash looked at her watch. "We'd better, if we still want to go to the cinema."

"Helen only offered to take us because she wants to see the new Pixar film but she thinks she's too grown up for it now," scoffed Dani. Her sister Helen was eighteen and in her final year at the school.

Tash laughed. "True, but I want to see it, and you know we can't go without someone from the Sixth Form." She reached out a flip-flopped foot and prodded Anisha.

"I can't wait until we're old enough to go into town without supervision," said Dani.

"What?" mumbled Anisha, looking around. "Did I fall asleep?"

"Only for a few minutes," said Tash. "Anyway," she added, looking back at Dani, "I wouldn't want to be in Helen's year yet. They're all auditioning for jobs at ballet companies – scary!"

"*And* they have to leave Aurora House in only two months' time," added Anisha. "They must feel so sad."

She shivered a little at the thought, and Tash was secretly pleased to see that Anisha loved school so much, when only last term it had seemed as if she was going off the idea of being a ballet dancer. They'd had important ballet exams just before Easter, and Anisha had found it so difficult to focus all term that she'd only just scraped through. Tash would never stop being thankful that they were all still here, dancing together every day.

She stood up and brushed some grass off her light blue dress. The others got up too, and the three of them walked back towards the mansion house that was the main school building.

"I really hope we find out about the end-of-year show soon," said Dani, padding across the grass in bare feet, carrying her pale-green Converse trainers in one hand and her French book in the other.

"We've been back at school for a week already and we don't know anything yet – we *must* be finding out soon," said Tash.

"You know, when we start rehearsals for the show we probably won't be able to carry on with dance club," said Anisha.

Tash realized Anisha was right. They'd started a Year Seven and Eight dance club last term so that everyone could have some fun and get their minds off their important ballet exams, and she felt a bit sad that they'd have to give it up to focus on the school show. But she couldn't feel sad for long, because she knew the end-of-year performance was going to be even more fun.

"I still can't believe we get to dance on the City Ballet stage!" she said.

City Ballet was the ballet company that the school was associated with, and it was Tash's dream to be a dancer there one day.

"I know!" grinned Dani. "It's going to be amazing."

Tash clapped her hands excitedly and Anisha skipped a few steps ahead in delight. They'd all come to Aurora House because they loved to dance, and because they wanted to make their ballerina dreams come true. Dancing on the stage where City Ballet performed would be one more step along the way.

"I wonder what we'll be dancing," said Anisha, turning back to face Dani and Tash.

"I hope it's something classical," said Tash.

"Me too," Dani agreed. "When I dance on that stage for the first time, I *really* want to be wearing a tutu!"

"Yeah, as long as it's in a tutu, I'll dance anything!" Tash said with a laugh.

She pictured the three of them standing in classical ballet positions like *arabesques* and *attitudes*, wearing the prettiest tutus she could imagine, lights shining down on them and the audience applauding. Just thinking about it made her do a little skipping step as they went in to get ready for the cinema.

Monday morning's ballet class started at the *barre* as usual, with everyone standing neatly in lines along the two mirrored sides of the big studio. They worked their way through *pliés*, *battements tendus*, *rondes de jambes* and *developpés*, bending and stretching and sweeping their arms through the main classical positions in time with their legs and feet. Then they moved on to faster exercises – quick *frappés* and finally *grands battements*, kicking their legs as high as they could.

The *barre* exercises took up the first hour and then the twelve girls in Tash's ballet class rearranged themselves into three lines in the middle of the studio to do centre exercises. Tash was in the back row and as she danced, she looked in the mirror and took in the sight of twelve young dancers whose movements matched just as perfectly as their navy-blue leotards, pink tights and soft, pink ballet shoes. They looked almost like the *corps de ballet* of a proper ballet company – the dancers who were often in the background, all dressed alike and doing exactly the same steps.

Sparkling Solo

They might not be the stars of the show, but Tash knew, from watching ballets on DVD and learning about the history of ballet at Aurora House, that the *corps de ballet* had one of the most important jobs of all. Without them, *Swan Lake* wouldn't be so breathtaking, there'd be no snowflakes or party guests in *The Nutcracker*, and *Giselle* wouldn't be anywhere near so creepy.

Although Tash didn't know what the end-of-year show would be, she didn't expect that she and her friends, as Year Sevens, would have big parts. But that didn't have to be so bad, she realized now, watching her ballet class move as if they shared one mind. To dance on that stage with her classmates, all of them breathing and moving in time with each other – well, it would really feel like being *part* of something. She'd loved ballet for years, but her friends at junior school hadn't been into it at all. Aurora House had taught her what it was like to love something that everyone around you loved just as much, and dancing with her friends here was the most special thing ever.

After the ballet class, they had twenty minutes to change into their navy-blue-and-grey school uniforms and get to their form room. Two whole terms of making the quick change had helped them all to get much faster, and Tash, Dani and Anisha no longer had to run to get there on time. They didn't arrive bright red in the face and with messy hair any more either.

Tash sat down next to Dani, and Anisha sat behind them with Donna, a pretty red-haired girl who was in their dormitory. They all started chatting about that morning's ballet class while the rest of their form – including the twelve boys, who had their morning dance classes separately – wandered in and sat down.

"Hurry up, hurry up," their form teacher Mr Kent said to the stragglers, but the chatter didn't die down. "Quiet please, Year Seven! Rob, put that away. Toril, looking at me, please. Come *on*,

Nick, we're all waiting for you."

Tash looked at the clock on the wall – they weren't running late, so she didn't know why he was making such a fuss. Mr Kent was usually relaxed and happy to let them chat while he did the register.

"We've got a special assembly this morning, so we're going to the auditorium instead of having form time," he explained. "Line up by the door, please. I'll do the register while we're there. Come on, Laura, leave your bag here, no one wants to be sitting next to a pair of smelly ballet shoes."

Tash looked at Dani, who looked back at her with hopeful blue eyes. Could this be the announcement about the end-of-year show?

Half the school was already sitting down by the time Year Seven arrived at the small theatre. A stage with proper theatrical lighting, wings and a curtain took up one end of the big room, and the rest was filled with tiered seating. Mr Kent led his form to the front two rows of seats and they sat down. Year Eight were already sitting in the two rows behind them. Tash's year shared a common room with them, so she knew most of them pretty well, and she and Anisha quickly joined the conversation Lucy and Chris from Year Eight were having behind them.

"It's got to be about the show," said Chris. "Ms Hartley's here, see." He pointed to the back of the stage where old Ms Hartley, the school's founder and a former principal dancer at City Ballet, was talking to Mr Watkins, the headteacher.

"Will we all be doing the same ballet?" Tash asked Chris and Lucy. "Or does each year do their own thing?"

"Last year each class did something different," said Lucy.

"And lots of the Sixth Form did solos or *pas de deux*," added Chris.

"I don't know what happened the year before that," said Lucy.

Tash turned round to ask Dani if she knew, but Dani was kneeling up on her seat, facing the back of the auditorium where the Sixth Form were sitting, and having a conversation with Helen through weird hand signs and mouthed words.

Ms Hartley walked forwards to the front of the stage and the noise died down. Tash tugged Dani back down into her seat.

"Good morning," Ms Hartley began. "It's lovely to see you all again. I know everyone is keen to know what this assembly is about, so I'll jump right into it. As most of you know, at the end of every year, the whole school puts on a performance at the City Ballet theatre. This will mark the end of a year of hard work for each of you, and for our graduating students, it will be their final performance as Aurora House dancers. This year, Aurora House Ballet School is fifty years old, and to celebrate this, we've decided that our performance must be incredibly special. I've told you all before that I named the school after the ballet role that made my name as a star dancer –

Aurora in *The Sleeping Beauty*. So, to celebrate the school, this year we will all be working towards one ballet. *That* ballet. *The Sleeping Beauty*."

Tash gave Dani a huge smile. On the other side of her she felt Anisha grab her arm in excitement, and she turned to grin at Anisha too.

The Sleeping Beauty was one of Tash's favourite ballets and she was thrilled that she'd get to dance in it!

"Of course, there are far more of you than there are parts," said Ms Hartley. "For that reason, and to give each year group a chance to shine onstage, we'll be splitting the ballet into sections."

She looked at Mr Watkins, who stepped forward to explain.

"Years Seven and Eight will perform the first scene," he said. "The baby Aurora is visited by fairies, and the wicked Carabosse curses her to prick her finger on a needle and die. The Lilac Fairy is able to save Aurora from death so that she will sleep for a hundred years instead."

"Oh, wow," breathed Tash.

She remembered watching City Ballet perform *The Sleeping Beauty* during the autumn half-term week. She'd been bowled over by the beautiful steps and lovely costumes, especially in the first scene and she was so glad that her class would be dancing it. She and Dani exchanged glances with sparkling eyes.

"Years Nine and Ten will then perform the garden scene, where the sixteen-year-old princess dances with princes and her friends before pricking her finger and falling into a deep sleep," Mr Watkins went on. "The 'vision scene', where the Lilac Fairy finds the Prince and shows him a vision of Aurora, and then leads him to kiss her, will be danced by Years Eleven and Twelve. This is a short scene, but, as those students all have important academic exams this summer, I'm sure they'll be glad not to have too much choreography to learn on top of school revision! Finally, the wedding scene is for Year Thirteen, our graduating students. If you've seen the ballet, as I know many of you have, you'll remember that there are lots of solo roles in this scene, so it's the perfect final showcase for them."

"Maybe Helen will get a solo!" Dani whispered. "How cool would that be?"

"Amazing!" Tash whispered back.

Mr Kent leaned forward in his seat at the end of the row and gave them both a look, so Tash went quiet and focused on Mr Watkins, who was still explaining how the show would work.

"Organizing things this way means that students from each year will have a chance to be given a solo," he said. "For example, someone from Year Seven or Eight will be the Lilac Fairy in the first scene, then someone in Year Nine or Ten will have that role in the second scene and so on. We'll do the same for the King and Queen, people in the palace, and Aurora's friends. There will be two exceptions to this. As Aurora was such an important role for Ms Hartley, we've decided to give one student here the chance to dance it throughout the whole ballet. The same will also apply to the role of the Prince. And those two roles will, of course, go to two of our final-year students."

Tash twisted her head to look over her shoulder at the back row where the eldest dancers sat, and thought about how special it would feel to be the one chosen to dance Aurora.

"Thank you for listening so patiently to all this," said Ms Hartley. "I can see that most of you are dying to talk about everything you've just heard, and my watch tells me it's time you were all on your way to your classrooms, so that will be all. You'll find out details of how the roles will be given out in your ballet classes, so don't ask me!"

The whole school started clapping, partly because they were so excited, and partly because they were sitting in a theatre and it felt like what you were supposed to do.

"Aaaahhh!" Tash squealed – she couldn't even form proper words. She grabbed Anisha's arm, bouncing up and down on the balls of her feet as they filed out.

"Do you think there's *any* chance someone in our year will get a solo?" asked Anisha.

"I don't know," replied Tash. "There are *loads* of good dancers in Year Eight."

"*But*," said Dani, bumping against Tash in her excitement, "there are also *loads* of solo roles in the first scene. All the fairies, and the King and Queen and stuff. Maybe there's a small chance. A tiny one."

"Do you think we'll get to dance in our pointe shoes?" asked Anisha.

Last term, the Year Seven girls had all got their first pair of pointe shoes – pink satin ballet shoes that were hard and flat at the ends so that they could dance on their toes. Or try to, anyway. They'd learned quite a lot in only a term because they practised every day, but they still had a long way to go before they could do any of the wonderful things they saw the older students doing. Tash wasn't at all sure that she was ready to dance *en pointe* onstage, and she guessed that if they *were* going to be dancing in pointe shoes, the Year Eight girls, who'd had an extra year of practice, would sweep up all the solo parts.

"Let's ask Miss Anderbel," she suggested, knowing that her favourite ballet teacher would have the answer.

"Oh, *why* do we not have a lesson with her until tomorrow morning?" wailed Anisha. "I can't wait that long!"

Tash was sure she couldn't either. It was only the beginning of the school day – they still had hours and hours of school lessons followed by a contemporary dance class and then a long evening of homework and games to drag out their suspense.

But as the day went on, she began to be glad that they hadn't been able to ask about roles. If Miss Anderbel said that the solos would all go to Year Eight, she knew she would still be happy to be in the *corps de ballet*, dancing on a famous stage alongside her friends. But until the parts were announced, she could dream of something even more special: dancing a solo.

And daydream she did – all the way through maths and French, geography and art, she danced the Lilac Fairy in her mind.

Chapter 2

"Miss Anderbel, what parts are we going to have in the show?" Dani burst out at the beginning of the Year Seven girls' ballet class the next morning.

"Will Year Eight get all of the solos?" asked Lily-May.

"Is there *any* chance that one of us might get one?" asked Donna.

Everyone looked at Miss Anderbel with hopeful eyes and Tash wished and wished that their teacher would say they might be lucky enough to get solo parts.

"If I tell you everything now, will you all stop asking me questions and focus on your exercises?" asked Miss Anderbel.

Everyone nodded hard and promised. Miss Anderbel paused and smiled at the class, and Tash felt like she might explode from the suspense of not knowing.

"You'll all have a chance to try out for the solo roles," Miss Anderbel continued.

Gasps and excited squeaks bounced off the mirrors that lined the studio. Tash turned around to grin at Anisha, who was standing behind her at the *barre*.

"I'm going to teach all of you the beginning of the Lilac Fairy's solo and part of the dramatic section where Carabosse the wicked fairy curses the baby Aurora to die," said Miss Anderbel. "Then there'll be an audition in your morning class next Monday. You'll each perform both pieces in the audition, and all of the solo roles will be cast based on your performances. There are five fairy solos, too, as well as the King and Queen, so there aren't just two opportunities to dance solos. Year Eight will be doing exactly the same thing, so you'll all have a fair chance."

"Only a week to learn it all?" Anisha murmured in a worried voice, and Tash pulled a scared face back at her. A week wasn't long at all to memorize steps and practise them until they were perfect enough to win one of the solo roles.

"Will we dance *en pointe*?" asked Laura, and everyone looked intently at their teacher for the answer.

"No," replied Miss Anderbel. "You've only been doing pointe work for a term and we've decided that, as your section of the ballet will be about twenty minutes long and most of you will be onstage for the whole scene, it's best if you dance in your flat shoes. Year Eight will be dancing in flat shoes, too, don't worry. I know some of you might be a bit disappointed as you want to show off your new skills to your parents and friends, but your safety is more important. Besides, we expect an extremely high standard of performance from all of you, and, although your pointe work is progressing well, I don't think it's quite ready for the stage yet."

Tash was surprised to feel so relieved. She'd had visions of herself dancing onstage in a tutu and pointe shoes, but she knew she'd stand a much better chance of getting a solo if she could dance in her soft, flat ballet shoes than she would doing beautiful but difficult pointe work. Miss Anderbel was right – dancing as well as they could was the most important thing, and until she'd had more practice in pointe shoes, that meant keeping things simple.

While they got on with their usual *barre* exercises, everyone at least pretended to focus on hard work instead of the performance. No one said anything more about it, but Tash couldn't stop herself *thinking* about it, and she guessed that everyone else was doing the same.

When they moved into the centre, they did a lovely new *port de bras* exercise and a pretty sequence of small jumps turning in different directions, which forced Tash to concentrate on what she was doing for five minutes at least. But as soon as she'd stopped jumping, her mind returned to *The Sleeping Beauty* and the audition next week. How was she ever going to learn the steps for two different parts well enough in just six days?

"Well, if any of you are going to get solos, we'd better start preparing for the audition, don't you think?" said Miss Anderbel with a smile.

They still had an hour of their morning ballet class left, which Miss Anderbel used to teach them the beginning of the Lilac Fairy's dance. She played them the music first.

Tash already knew it by heart. She'd always adored the Lilac Fairy's solo – to dance to this music on the City Ballet stage would be a dream come true. And the next thing that Miss Anderbel said made her even more desperate to win the role.

"Because you'll be dancing in flat shoes, and that makes the steps much easier, for the Year Seven and Eight section we've decided to use most of the original choreography, which is over one hundred years old and is performed by ballet companies across the world. We'll adapt it a little, of course, so that it works for flat shoes, and we'll shorten it because the real ballet is pretty long! But generally speaking, all of you will be dancing the real *Sleeping Beauty* choreography, whether that's a solo or in a group dance."

Tash felt a fluttering like fairy wings in her stomach. If she could only do well in the audition, she might have a chance – a tiny, small, minuscule chance – of dancing the famous Lilac Fairy solo on the City Ballet stage!

The section for the audition was very short,

and when Miss Anderbel demonstrated the steps, it looked quite easy.

It wasn't.

They had to start in one of the back corners of the studio and dance in a diagonal line across the floor to the opposite front corner. There were only a handful of steps, repeated four times – a *developpé* to second, where Miss Anderbel wanted them to unfold their left leg as high as they could while making sure it was straight and perfectly turned out. Then it was some sweeping turns to face the other corner and back again, and finally an *arabesque* on *demi-pointe* with the front arm held triumphantly high, and a skip forwards to begin the sequence again.

Once they'd learned that and practised it a lot, Miss Anderbel added the next bit: travelling backwards along the same diagonal line, stepping through *attitudes* and *arabesques* and spinning around in double *pirouettes* with their arms rounded above their heads.

"Your arms should be grand and sweeping, moving all the time," said Miss Anderbel. "But the movements should be open and gentle, too. The Lilac Fairy knows she has a lot of magical power, but at the same time she wants to use it all for good, to protect the baby Aurora."

Tash nodded, and tried to remember that as she practised the steps again. It was difficult to get the steps right and to get the *feeling* of the steps right at the same time! And of course the whole thing had to flow perfectly along with the music, too. Whenever Tash had seen it performed by professional ballerinas it had looked nothing but lovely and effortless – and they'd been doing it all *en pointe*! To Tash, even in flat shoes, dancing it felt the absolute opposite of lovely.

She tried hard not to watch herself in the mirror. Every time she caught a glimpse, she could see what a mess the steps looked when she did them. She tried to tell herself that she'd only just learned the dance so of course it didn't look perfect yet. But she knew that if she was going to get the part, she'd have to get better at it very quickly.

"That's all we're going to learn for the audition," Miss Anderbel said, when she'd watched them perform the steps in two groups. Tash was glad to see that no one was dancing them effortlessly yet, although Lily-May was closer than anyone else. "We'll go through it again tomorrow, and I'll teach you all a bit of Carabosse, too."

Tash grabbed her bottle of water and gulped some down.

"That's *hard*," said Anisha, as they walked out to the changing room together.

"I feel like I need a week to get the steps right in my mind and then another week to get them right in my feet," said Dani. "And we only have a week for all of it!"

"I like the backwards bit," said Tash. "It's easier than that horrible *developpé*."

Tash had worried so much about getting

pirouettes right in her first term at Aurora House, but now she could do them with confidence. She was glad that she'd get a chance to show her teachers how well she could do doubles.

"I wish we could choose which part we want to audition for," said Anisha. "I'd go for Carabosse and give up all this good-fairy nonsense."

"It's not nonsense!" cried Dani. "It's *beautiful*."

"I agree about choosing parts, though," said Tash. "I don't want to do Carabosse at all."

"You're both nuts," said Anisha. "That's going to be the most fun part. It's the only one with any real acting, anyway."

"It's all yours," said Tash. "I only want to be the Lilac Fairy."

"Yesterday you said you didn't mind as long as you got a tutu," said Dani.

"And now that I know it's going to be the actual choreography, and that we might have a chance, I don't mind as long as my tutu is lilac," Tash replied with a laugh.

She knew that the Lilac Fairy was a long shot. But she was going to give it all she had.

"Tash, what did I just say?" Mr Kent asked halfway through that afternoon's English lesson, interrupting her in the middle of going through the Lilac Fairy steps in her mind.

"Um…Mister Tom…the war…I don't know," Tash admitted.

"Please try to get your brain out of the ballet studio and into the classroom. I know the end-of-year performance is important to you all, but I hope I don't need to remind you that your end-of-year *exams* are coming up soon too. They're first in the calendar and they should also be first in your minds."

"Sorry," murmured Tash.

She pulled her book, which had almost slipped off the desk, back towards her and glanced over at Dani to see what page they were on. She'd daydreamed her way through three pages of the story so she quickly flicked to the right place, and Dani pushed her notebook across the table so that Tash could copy what her friend had written down about the pages she'd missed.

"Thanks," she mouthed to Dani, who smiled back at her. Tash looked around the classroom. Everyone *seemed* to be paying attention, but she couldn't believe that she was the only one whose feet were tracing ballet steps under the table, or whose mind was far away on the City Ballet stage.

That evening, Tash and her friends sat in the common room together doing some homework. After she'd been caught out by Mr Kent, Tash had remembered how important it was to do well in the school exams and keep her scholarship, and she'd promised herself that she'd start working much harder in academic lessons.

Year Seven had already had their supervised homework time, and Tash had finished almost everything, but she thought it would be a good idea to get started on the English homework that wasn't due in until next week. She wanted to make it really good so that Mr Kent would see that she was trying. But it was difficult to focus when all she could think about was how hard the Lilac Fairy solo was, and how she only had a week to get it perfect before the audition.

She was using her laptop to work on the myth story that Mr Kent had asked them to write, and it was almost too easy to open up YouTube and search for ballet videos. There were loads of versions of the Lilac Fairy, including a few City Ballet ones – there was even one of Miss Anderbel dancing it years ago!

Tash plugged her iPod headphones into her computer so that the music wouldn't disturb Dani and Anisha, and watched every video she could find. She paused them and watched the opening section again and again, trying to fix the arm movements and flowing grace in her mind so that her own body might do the same thing.

She sighed. They were all so, so perfect and she was so far away from being as good.

She'd lost count of how many different videos she'd watched when she realized that it was getting late and would soon be time for bed. And she'd only written two sentences of her myth story! She looked around. Dani and Anisha were both reading *Goodnight Mister Tom* and so were a few of their other friends, which reminded Tash that she needed to finish reading it too. Some people were watching TV or playing games and chatting, and that made Tash feel a bit better – she had ages and ages to get the English homework done, after all. She didn't *need* to do it right now.

She pulled her headphones out of her ears and was about to shut her laptop down when a movement on Lily-May's screen caught her eye: the Lilac Fairy. Lily-May was doing exactly the same thing Tash was! She was obviously determined to get the role, too. Tash hesitated. Lily-May was *good*, maybe the best dancer in their year.

Sparkling Solo

If Tash was going to have any chance of dancing the Lilac Fairy, she was going to have to beat Lily-May *and* the Year Eight girls to it. She put her headphones back in.

One more video, and then she'd get on with the book. Just one more.

Chapter 3

The next day, Tash's class worked on the Lilac Fairy solo again, and they learned part of the role of Carabosse too. It turned out to be a lot more fun than Tash thought it would be. She still desperately wanted to be the Lilac Fairy, but learning the sequence of acting steps and gestures where the wicked fairy curses the baby princess was hilarious. Everyone pulled the most evil faces they could manage, pretending that they had long claw-like fingernails and were filled with hatred for the good fairies. Laura and Dani both made everyone laugh a lot, but Anisha was the scariest. Tash thought that she wouldn't be at all surprised if Anisha was given the role when it came to the audition.

Tash got into the fun as much as anyone, but part of her mind was always on the Lilac Fairy solo, and when they were given time to practise both roles by themselves the next day, she spent all her time on the solo she was hoping to be dancing for the rest of term. She'd been spending every spare moment watching videos of famous dancers performing the solo, and she really felt as if she was beginning to understand how it should look. She'd watched some of them so many times that she saw them in her mind when she closed her eyes at night, and when she stared out of the window in her school lessons.

She didn't *mean* to daydream so much when she was meant to be listening to her teachers or working through a set of textbook questions, but somehow it just kept on happening. One minute she'd be paying attention to a lesson on fractions and the next she'd be away with the fairies – away *as one of* the fairies. Unfortunately, her teachers had started to notice.

"Who can tell me what the answer to number one should be?" Miss Hewett asked in Friday morning's maths lesson. "Tash?"

Tash blinked and focused her eyes on the board, dragging her mind back from the ballet studio.

"Um…" She fumbled around her brain for the answer, but all she found there were ballet steps. "One and a half?"

Miss Hewett frowned. "We went over this ten minutes ago. Weren't you listening?"

Tash went bright red, and didn't say anything. She hadn't been able to concentrate on anything school-related all week; all she could think about was the audition on Monday. She read what was on the board again and forced her mind to work.

"Two quarters," she finally said, almost sure that she was right.

"Which is…?" asked Miss Hewett impatiently.

"Oh! One half," said Tash.

"Correct. One half. Please pay more attention, Tash. This is going to be in your exam."

Tash sighed and nodded. She rested her chin in her hand and Anisha gave her a sympathetic smile. Tash resolved not to think about ballet at all for the rest of the lesson, but it was so difficult to keep her mind away from dancing.

By Sunday evening, excitement and nerves about the audition were building up in the Year Seven and Eight common room, and Tash gave up all her efforts to think about anything else.

"Let's practise," suggested Sarah from Year Eight.

They all helped move the sofas and chairs to the sides of the room, and Chris plugged in his iPod for music. Sarah scrolled through and found what she was looking for.

"Lilac Fairy first!" she said. "But I don't think we can all dance at once…"

Half of the girls, including Dani, found a space in the middle of the room and started dancing along with the music.

Tash sat on the back of a sofa that had been pushed against the wall, next to Anisha and Toril. As she watched, Tash realized that a lot of the older girls were really, really good and she tried to remind herself that she shouldn't get her hopes up; they would probably get all the fairy solos, as well as Carabosse and the King and Queen, and one of them would almost definitely be the Lilac Fairy.

Dani was dancing near the back of the room, and at first she was doing really well. But just when she was nearly finished, she muddled her feet up and did an *arabesque* on the wrong leg. Tash saw her friend's sunny smile turn instantly into a frown.

When the music ended, Dani flopped down

onto the sofa at Tash's feet and buried her face in a cushion. "I'm going to do so badly tomorrow!" she wailed.

"It's probably just nerves," Tash said, patting her friend on the back as she climbed down to the floor and found a space to dance just in front.

Anisha slid down onto the sofa and Dani sat up.

"I totally messed up the last bit," said Dani. "There aren't even that many steps! And I *still* managed to get it wrong."

"Don't think about it," said Anisha. "Once you're doing it properly tomorrow, I'm sure you'll be fine."

It was hard to do a proper diagonal across the floor when there were so many other people in the way, but Tash did the best she could. No one had space to do any of the *developpés* or *arabesques* properly, but it felt good to dance in time with the music and with everyone else. After four ballet lessons just practising the same tiny bit of the dance again and again, Tash no longer felt messy when she did the steps. She felt graceful and light and she knew that she'd be able to smile while she danced in the audition; she loved the dance so much that she wouldn't be able to *stop* smiling!

The next morning, everyone in Coppélia dorm got dressed quickly and did their hair extra carefully. No one wanted their hair to come down from its ballet bun halfway through the audition!

"What are you *doing*?" Tash asked Anisha, catching her pulling faces in the mirror.

"I'm practising for Carabosse," replied Anisha, as if it was obvious, and Tash realized that it really should have been.

"Tash, why is your English book under my bed?" asked Laura.

"Oh, I don't know," said Tash, taking the book without stopping the Lilac Fairy arm movements she was practising. "Who cares about *that* now?"

"Mr Kent will, if you don't have it in the lesson," Dani reminded her.

"True," sighed Tash.

But that moment was all the time she would give to thoughts of English lessons. This morning was *all* about *The Sleeping Beauty*.

The audition was in their morning ballet class, so after breakfast they headed along the path through the gardens to the modern block of studios in the school grounds. When they got there, they found Miss Anderbel, Mr Watkins and Ms Hartley waiting for them. Tash and her friends exchanged nervous glances; they hadn't expected the school's founder to be watching them! To their surprise, the boys from their year were there too.

Miss Anderbel led them through some warm-up exercises at the *barre*, but if she'd been asked what they were afterwards, Tash wouldn't have had a clue. Her mind was running through the Lilac Fairy while her feet and arms did what Miss Anderbel asked of them.

At last, they were ready to start. Miss Anderbel told them all to sit along the side of the room and wait until it was their turn to dance. The boys went first. The main solo roles for them were the Lilac Fairy's partner, the partners to the other fairies, and the King. They'd all learned some of the King's steps and acting sequences, and then they had to dance part of the role of the Lilac Fairy's partner. The steps had been simplified for them – boys didn't ever dance *en pointe* so the real male ballet steps couldn't be made easier for them by just dancing in flat shoes! They danced in groups of three, so Tash guessed that the girls would do the same.

"At least we don't have to dance completely by ourselves!" Dani whispered to her, and Tash nodded.

Tash watched the boys dance with only half her attention; the rest was on what she'd have to do when it was her turn. She'd been excited about the audition all weekend, but now she felt a bit sick. She replayed all the videos she could remember in her mind and tried to think about all the little details those other dancers had put in to make their dancing perfect.

It seemed no time at all before the boys were finished and the girls were up. Anisha was in the first group, and she performed Carabosse better than she ever had before. Her Lilac Fairy was quite good, too, but she had obviously put all her energy into preparing for Carabosse; she hardly seemed to have practised the Lilac Fairy, and Tash spotted a few places where she could have been neater.

Dani was next, and Tash gave her hand a quick squeeze. Dani walked shakily out to the middle of the room with the rest of her group and began with Carabosse. She did everything correctly, but it didn't have quite as much sparkle as usual. Tash guessed that Dani was more nervous than before because she'd messed things up when they were practising in the common room. It was weird to see her confident best friend like this – Dani hadn't even seemed as nervous as this in the ballet exam last term. But this was a performance, and somehow, even though the exam had been important, this seemed to matter more. Tash watched her, willing her to do better.

She *did* manage to do much better on the Lilac Fairy. The music seemed to energize her, enough for her usual sparkling smile to appear, and she danced the steps beautifully. Once she'd got past the *arabesque* that she'd messed up in the common room, her dancing shone even more, and she performed the last few steps with her head held high. Tash was relieved; she wanted her friends to do well almost as much as she wanted to do well herself. When Dani sat back down next to her, Tash gave her a quick sideways hug, but there was no time to speak. She was next.

Tash stood in the middle of the room with Toril and Donna, and waited for Miss Anderbel to start the Carabosse music. The table where the three teachers sat seemed very far away. Miss Anderbel's usual lovely smile was replaced by a very serious expression, and Mr Watkins and Ms Hartley had never looked so stern before. Tash swallowed to clear her dry throat.

The music started and Tash moved with it, her body doing the evil fairy's mime actions automatically. It took a few seconds for her brain to catch up. For the first moment, it was like she was watching herself dancing from outside. But then she realized where she was: an audition! Even if Carabosse wasn't the part she really wanted, she might as well try her best. She wanted to show her teachers that she was able to do lots of different things well.

The piece was soon over, and she looked hopefully at the teachers to see what they thought. But their expressions gave nothing away at all.

"Thanks, girls," said Miss Anderbel. "Now the Lilac Fairy."

Tash walked with the others to the back corner of the studio and stood on her left foot in the starting position, with her right foot pointed behind her, and her right arm lifted towards the ceiling while her left arm was held out to the side. Miss Anderbel pressed play.

Tash's feet and arms were swept along by the wonderful music, through the steps that so many dancers had performed before her, and she flowed through the melody, feeling so much a part of it that she didn't think she'd be able to stop dancing, even if Miss Anderbel told her to.

She'd practised the steps so many times in the last week that she was able to do even the difficult first part of the solo much better than she could when they first learned it. She smiled as she stepped into *arabesques* and turned beautiful *pirouettes*. Even if she never got to dance these steps again, she was dancing them *now*, and for a moment, that was almost enough.

The music stopped and Tash finished dancing.

"Thank you," said Mr Watkins, but she couldn't tell anything from his tone.

"Well done," Dani whispered when she sat back down. "That was really good."

"Thanks," Tash whispered back.

She wouldn't say it out loud because she didn't want to jinx her chances, but it had *felt* good. She'd felt elegant and strong, grand and gentle, just like Miss Anderbel had said they should be.

Tash watched the last group anxiously. She knew it wasn't likely that anyone in Year Seven would get to be the Lilac Fairy, but if she was going to have a chance, she needed to be better than the others. Lily-May was in this group, and by the time she'd finished, she'd taken all Tash's hope away. She was amazing. She danced better than she ever had in class, and even though Tash had danced her best too, she had a horrible feeling that wasn't enough to beat Lily-May.

"When do you think we'll find out?" Tash asked her friends on their way to English.

They'd asked Miss Anderbel at the end of the

audition but she'd only said that it wouldn't be until all the parts had been decided.

"Not until Year Eight have had their audition this afternoon, anyway," said Anisha.

"I guess we shouldn't get our hopes up," said Dani. "I bet I wasn't good enough for a solo."

"You don't know that," said Tash. "You did the Lilac Fairy really well."

"Anyway," said Anisha, "we'll still get to dance on the City Ballet stage, even if we don't have solos."

"Helen had one when she was in Year Seven," said Dani.

"That proves it, then!" Tash said brightly. "Year Sevens *can* get solos."

"Yeah, if your name is Helen Taylor," said Dani, and there was a gloomy note in her voice that showed she didn't think the same luck would apply to her.

Tash didn't understand why Dani was being so negative, and she exchanged a worried look with Anisha. Everyone was anxious about what parts they'd be given, but whenever the whole class was worried about something, it was usually Dani who could see the sunny side of things. For once, Tash was glad they had an English lesson to go to – at least that would help them all to stop thinking about the audition.

Chapter 4

As soon as they got to English, Mr Kent asked them all to hand in their myth stories.

"I'm really looking forward to reading these," he said as Laura went around the classroom collecting them. Tash handed hers over with a feeling of dread. She knew she hadn't spent enough time on it and Mr Kent was definitely going to be disappointed when he read it. But there was nothing she could do about it now. And, anyway, if she hadn't tried her very hardest at the story, it was only because the audition was so important. Mr Kent would understand that.

Once Mr Kent had glanced through the pile of papers to check that everyone had handed something in, he put his students in groups and gave them each a topic relating to *Goodnight Mister Tom* to discuss and then tell the rest of the class about. Tash was put with Nick, Rob and Dani. They were supposed to be talking about the theme of growing up in the book, but all they could think of was the audition and who the solo roles would be given to.

"It's pointless talking about it," mumbled Dani. "We didn't see the Year Eights' auditions so we don't know how they did."

"Yes, but if you had to cast the roles just from our year?" insisted Rob.

"Tash for Lilac Fairy," Dani said immediately.

Tash smiled at her, but she felt sure Dani was just saying it because she was her best friend.

"No, Lily-May, definitely," Tash said.

"I'm with Dani," said Nick. "I think it should be you."

"Thanks," smiled Tash.

She caught sight of Mr Kent heading their way so she quickly changed the subject back to the book. "So. Growing up. And stuff." She bent her head over her book so it would look as if she was reading it closely.

"Oh yes, good point, Tash, growing up," said Dani, pretending to be very serious.

Tash couldn't help giggling, and by the time she looked up again, Mr Kent had gone to talk to Anisha's group. They didn't have much longer until they had to speak in front of the rest of the class, so they spent five minutes coming up with some things they could say about their topic, but that was all the concentration they could manage before they went back to casting their Year Seven Only version of *The Sleeping Beauty*.

* * *

They had to wait four whole days to find out the real casting. They asked Miss Anderbel at the beginning of every ballet lesson if the teachers had made their decision, and on Tuesday, Wednesday and Thursday, she said no. On Friday morning, when they walked into the studio, she was waiting for them with a big smile on her face.

"Is it decided yet?" asked Anisha.

She didn't even need to say what she was talking about – the casting for the performance was the only thing on anyone's mind.

"It is," replied Miss Anderbel, her smile getting even bigger as she spoke.

Tash knew she shouldn't expect anything and she didn't want dancing on the City Ballet stage to be ruined by feeling disappointed with her part. But she couldn't help a tiny feeling of hope fluttering inside her. There was a chance. So small it was almost invisible, but it was definitely there.

"I'm pleased to tell you that a few members of

this class have been given solos," Miss Anderbel went on.

The entire class gasped and everyone looked around at each other, trying to guess who it would be. Quite a few people looked at Tash and she felt her face heating up under their eyes. She didn't want anyone to look at her. She didn't want any of them to see how disappointed she'd be if she wasn't one of the girls chosen for a solo.

"The King and Queen will be Chris and Sarah in Year Eight," said Miss Anderbel.

Tash ticked those roles off the list in her mind. "Carabosse will be Lucy in Year Eight," Miss Anderbel continued.

Tash and Dani both gave Anisha sympathetic grimaces. Anisha shrugged at them a little sadly.

"I'm sorry, Anisha," said Miss Anderbel with a kind smile. "It was very close between you and Lucy, and I'd like you to learn the role as Lucy's understudy."

"Thanks!" said Anisha, and her whole face brightened.

"Fairies," Miss Anderbel continued, "Emma, Juliet and Poppy from the year above, and from this class, Lily-May and Dani."

Dani gasped and turned to Tash with a look of total shock on her face. Tash was so pleased for her friend, but it was hard to look as excited as she should. There was only the Lilac Fairy left, which meant that she probably hadn't got a solo at all. She hugged Dani quickly and then forced herself to look back at her teacher and hear who would be dancing the role she had desperately wanted for herself.

"The Lilac Fairy was very difficult to choose," said Miss Anderbel. "There were a few people who came very close, in this class and in Year Eight, but in the end we chose the person who we know will work hard all term and who we feel will bring just the right style and joy to the role. And that's you, Tash."

Tash stood still and her dark brown eyes went as wide as they could go. It took a few seconds for her to smile, she was so surprised. Had Miss Anderbel really said her name?

"Me?" she whispered to Dani, in case she'd heard wrong.

"Of course you!" Dani giggled.

"Do you think you're up to it, Tash?" Miss Anderbel asked, looking a bit worried at Tash's shocked reaction. "It'll be a lot of dancing. The Lilac Fairy is the main role in the first scene. You'll have the solo, but also some acting sections, and you'll be centre stage for most of the scene."

"Yes," Tash whispered.

She felt Dani nudge her in the side and realized that her answer must have been too quiet for anyone to hear.

"Yes, Miss Anderbel," she said again, much louder. "Yes, thank you! I'm so happy!"

"Good," Miss Anderbel smiled. "I had a suspicion you wouldn't turn it down."

Tash grinned at her, and then at her friends. She couldn't believe it!

"The rest of you will be the Lilac Fairy's attendants," said Miss Anderbel, "so you'll have a group dance to learn, which we'll start work on next week. Laura and Donna, I'd like you both to be understudies for the fairy solos."

Laura and Donna grinned at each other, and a murmur of happiness went around the rest of the class. They all knew that the Lilac Fairy's attendants would get to wear lovely purple tutus, and they were still excited about dancing on the City Ballet stage, even if they didn't have solos.

"I'm so proud that one of *us* got the part of the Lilac Fairy over the Year Eights!" Anisha said to Tash, and Donna and Toril, who were standing nearby, nodded in agreement.

"What about the boys?" Laura asked their teacher.

"Rob will be the Lilac Fairy's partner," said Miss Anderbel. "And Jonah will partner Dani.

The other fairies' partners will be boys from Year Eight, and the rest of the Year Seven boys will be Carabosse's evil minions."

The class laughed and Tash exchanged a happy smile with Dani. They both had solos, and now they knew they'd be dancing with two of the boys they were friends with as well. Everything was turning out perfectly. Well, almost.

Tash looked at Anisha to see how she felt. She wished that her other best friend had a solo, too, then all three of them could be just as happy as each other. But Anisha hardly seemed sad at all.

"You okay?" Tash asked her quietly.

Anisha nodded. "I'm just glad we'll be rehearsing for a performance this term and not working towards boring dance exams, and it'll be fun to learn the part of Carabosse properly, even if I never get to perform it. Plus, I suppose we have to leave some of the main roles for the Year Eights, or they might never let us choose what we want to watch on TV in the common room ever again."

Sparkling Solo

Tash was relieved to see that Anisha could already joke about it. If Anisha had been unhappy about not having a solo, Tash would have felt bad about having one herself.

"Who's going to be Aurora?" Dani asked.

She knew most of Year Thirteen because of her sister. Everyone turned eager eyes on their teacher. Even though no one else knew the oldest students as well as Dani, they were all dying to know who would be the star of the show.

"Aurora herself won't be finding out until the ballet class after yours, so I don't think it would be fair to tell you lot first," replied Miss Anderbel. "But if you ask your sister at lunchtime, I imagine she'll tell you." She smiled at Dani, and then clapped her hands together, switching into hard-work mode. "Right then, to the *barre*, everyone!"

Tash, Dani and Anisha hung around by the door to the dining room after they'd finished eating lunch. They could see Dani's sister Helen chatting to her friends while they took their trays to the racks at one end of the room.

When the older girls finally came towards them, walking with the pure grace of ballet dancers, Tash was suddenly aware that she was slouching a little against the wall and she stood up straighter. She wanted to be just as elegant as them one day.

"Helen!" cried Dani, grabbing hold of her sister's arm when she was close enough. "Who's Aurora?"

"Hmm, I'm not sure if I should give that information to nosy Year Sevens," Helen said, smirking.

"But you should give it to your adoring little sister," said Dani. "Come on, *please*. We're *desperate* to know."

"Well, if you're *desperate*," said Helen, smiling to show that she was only kidding. "I'll tell you. But only because I've been dying to tell you anyway. I've been looking out for you all morning."

"Who is it?" pleaded Dani.

Helen paused and grinned, dragging out the suspense. Tash and Anisha looked at her just as eagerly as Dani.

"It's me," said Helen.

Dani screamed and jumped up, hugging her sister so hard she almost knocked her down.

"Dani! Shhh!" warned Tash with a giggle, glancing around to see if other people were looking at them.

"*My sister* is going to be *Aurora!*" said Dani, when she finally let Helen go. "This is the coolest thing *ever.*"

"Pretty much," agreed Helen. She laughed and then pulled Dani back towards her for another ecstatic hug. "I'm *so* happy."

Tash looked at her in awe. Helen seemed so tall and grown up. She had long blonde hair like Dani, which was currently pulled back into a perfect bun, and even just standing still, her posture was strong, confident and controlled.

She looked every inch a professional ballerina.

"So what did you guys get?" Helen asked.

"Fairy solo," said Dani.

"Awesome!" cried Helen and she and Dani high-fived each other.

"Tash is going to be the Lilac Fairy," said Dani.

"Wow, well done," said Helen, smiling at Tash.

Tash felt butterflies in her stomach at the thought that the older students would notice her as the dancer who had been chosen for the main role in Year Seven and Eight. It felt special, but it also made her nervous. She knew she had a lot to live up to.

"Have you told Mum and Dad yet?" Dani asked Helen.

"No. Have you?"

"Nope. I was gonna call them later."

"Let's not," said Helen suddenly. "They're coming down next weekend to take us out for lunch anyway. Let's tell them then! It'll be a surprise. Both of us dancing solos!"

Dani grinned up at her sister and hugged her again.

Tash imagined how pleased their parents would be and how much fun Dani would have surprising them, but she knew she couldn't wait that long to tell Mum about her own solo.

"Mum, Mum, guess what?" Tash gushed, as soon as her mum answered the phone that evening.

"What?" laughed Mum.

"I've got a solo in the school show!" said Tash. "Not just any solo. I'm going to be the Lilac Fairy. It's the main part in the scene my year are performing."

"Wow! That's fantastic! Well done, Tash. I'm so proud of you."

"I'll let you know when you can get a ticket so that you can get a good seat. It's going to be in the City Ballet theatre! Can you believe that?"

"Oh, that's wonderful!"

"Mum, are you crying?"

"No, no…well, just a tiny bit. I'm so proud of you."

"*Mum!*" Tash laughed, but she couldn't help feeling thrilled at Mum's reaction. And she couldn't wait for Mum to watch her dance the solo that she alone had been chosen for out of all of the Year Seven and Eight girls.

But she also knew how difficult it was going to be. Miss Anderbel had already warned her that there would be a lot to learn, and as she thought about performing on that famous stage with a huge audience, dancing an important role in a show to celebrate fifty years of her school, she felt the pressure starting to build already.

"I'm so happy we will all dance together!" Toril said in her Norwegian-accented English when they were getting into bed that night.

"Me too," agreed Anisha. "And I'm so proud to be a Coppélia dorm girl. The bedroom of *two* Year Seven soloists!"

Tash and Dani grinned at each other.

"I wonder what our costumes will be like," wondered Donna.

"We'll all have the same. Purple tutus, I guess," said Laura. "Tash, *yours* will probably be super special to make it stand out from ours."

A thrill ran through Tash at the thought of dancing in a beautiful tutu. But she wouldn't let the dream of glitter and fairy dust take over. She had a lot of work to do before she got to the stage.

"Dani, can I borrow your iPad?" she asked, as the others snuggled down under the covers, probably already picturing themselves dancing across the stage in matching tutus.

"It's lights out in a minute," said Dani.

"I'll be quiet," promised Tash, and Dani handed her the iPad from her bedside table.

"Thanks," whispered Tash.

"Ready everyone?" asked Laura, standing at the light switch by the door.

"No, wait, my pillow's fallen on the floor!"

squealed Anisha, leaning down to grab it and put it back into place on her bed. "Okay, ready!" she called.

Laura turned the lights off and got back into her bed. "Night, everyone," she said.

"Night," murmured Anisha and Dani.

"Goodnight, fairies and fairy attendants," said Toril, and Tash smiled to herself in the dark.

She pulled the covers up over her head, put her headphones in her ears, and turned the iPad on, quickly tapping in Dani's password. She opened YouTube and found her favourite Lilac Fairy video. She had a lot of learning to do if she was ever going to be as good as the other dancers who had been the Lilac Fairy before her.

Chapter 5

On Monday morning, Miss Anderbel led Tash's class through a short warm-up at the *barre*, and then asked Tash, Dani and Lily-May to carry on working through their usual class exercises while she taught the rest of the group the beginning of their dance as the Lilac Fairy attendants.

"What shall we do now?" asked Lily-May, when they'd finished the *barre* exercises they usually did.

"We could do the *port de bras* from last week," suggested Dani.

"I think I'm going to go through the beginning of the Lilac Fairy," said Tash.

She found a space at one end of the room and began to practise the steps they'd learned for the audition. She was so excited about learning the rest of the dance that she couldn't think about anything else. Her turn would be coming soon!

"Your hands are wrong," said Lily-May, breaking into her happy thoughts.

Tash looked worriedly at her arms, where they were still held out in second.

"In all the videos and performances *I've* seen, it looks more like this," said Lily-May, putting her arms out to the sides in second position but with her wrists and hands curved more downwards than Tash's.

"Oh," said Tash.

She tried to adjust her hands and arms to the way Lily-May had held hers. It felt a bit weird, but maybe it was right. Lily-May didn't have time to say anything more, and Dani didn't have a chance to leap to Tash's defence – as Tash could see she was about to – because at that moment Miss Anderbel called the two of them over to begin learning the dance the fairies would do together before their solos.

The rest of the class had been sent to the back of the studio to practise what they'd learned so far. Tash caught Anisha's eye and smiled at her, and then she went back to rehearsing her own steps.

After Miss Anderbel had finished with Lily-May and Dani, she sent them away to practise too, and Tash walked to the middle of the studio with a big smile, completely ready to learn more of her solo. They went through the first section again, slowly, and it was so brilliant to be getting one-to-one coaching that Tash didn't even mind that she wasn't learning anything new yet. She tried to remember to hold her arms the way Lily-May had shown her. Miss Anderbel didn't correct it, or tell her to put them back the way she'd had them before, so Tash assumed that Lily-May must have been right. She decided that she'd ask Lily-May which videos she'd been watching so that she could pick up some more tips.

Once Miss Anderbel was happy that the first bit was coming along nicely, they moved on to the steps that followed: a pretty, fairy-light sequence where Tash had to *couru* across the floor, rising up onto *demi-pointe* and taking tiny, tiny steps as fast as she could, keeping her feet tightly together in fifth position. It was meant to look as if she was gliding across the stage, and the wafty, flowing arm movements that went with it made Tash feel just as if she was floating on fairy wings through the air.

Next came some *sissonne* jumps; big leaps where Tash's left leg flew out behind her so that it was like doing an *arabesque* in the air before she landed on the front foot and quickly closed the back leg in behind her in fifth position. Then she had to take off into a second flying leap, before spinning round in a double *pirouette*. When she came down from the *pirouette* she had to go straight into another *sissonne*, repeating the whole sequence again! It was so difficult to get it all right and to make it flow like one effortless dance, and by the end of the lesson Tash still couldn't manage it. She was disappointed, and she was suddenly afraid. She'd wanted the part of the Lilac Fairy so much. But what if she couldn't do it?

"Tash, come here," said Miss Anderbel.

Tash shuffled across the floor to her teacher. "Why do you think we chose you for the Lilac Fairy?"

"I don't know," replied Tash. "Because I managed to do okay in the audition?"

"Yes, but not just that. We looked at how everyone danced in the audition closely, of course, because it was a test of your nerves. But we've also been watching you all every day for the last two terms. So we know that you can dance well, not just in an audition, but every day in class. It's a difficult solo, Tash. You can't expect to do it perfectly right away."

"I know," sighed Tash. "I just hoped…"

"…that somehow you *would*?" guessed Miss Anderbel.

"Yes," said Tash with a laugh.

She realized that she was being silly, but she couldn't shake off her wish that she could do better.

"You'll get the steps soon," said Miss Anderbel. "I really believe that. We wouldn't have given you the part if we didn't think you could do it. So don't let your worry over that stop your personality from shining through. The lovely smile you always have when you dance is one of the reasons we chose you. The Lilac Fairy is like the narrator of the ballet. She has to really connect with the audience and draw them into the world of the fairy tale. And I can't think of *anyone* better to do that than you."

Tash went back out to the changing room with a big smile on her face and a warm feeling in her heart, and began to change into her school uniform.

"Miss Anderbel said we have to start doing some extra rehearsals with the Year Eight fairies soon," said Dani, "so that we can learn the dance together and sort out the spacing and stuff. I guess you'll be coming to those, too, Tash. You're in most of the fairy dances with us!"

"Sounds great," said Tash. "What's your group dance like?" she asked Anisha.

"Brilliant," said Anisha. "I can't wait to carry on with it tomorrow."

"The group fairy dance *is* lovely," added Dani, "but I really want to get started on my solo!"

All week, Miss Anderbel worked with the Year Sevens on their group dances and solos, and by the end of Friday, Tash was really starting to get the hang of the new section she'd learned. Dani was getting on well with her solo too. Tash stopped practising at the back of the studio for a while to watch her friend, and she was so pleased that Dani had been given the part.

Dani was often loud and cheeky, but she was great at light, delicate ballet steps and quick jumps, so she could be very fairy-like when she danced, especially because she was so small for her age. Tash watched her friend glide through the slow movements of the solo. She just *knew* that Dani was loving every second of this as much as she was.

"That's nice, Dani," Miss Anderbel said, as Dani almost shone with happiness while drifting through airy *balancés* and pretty *pas de bourrées*.

Tash smiled to herself and went back to practising her own solo. They might have school exams in a month, but that wasn't going to stop this being the best term ever.

"I love this so much," Dani said at the end of the lesson, sinking down onto the bench in the changing room beside Tash and Anisha.

"I know the feeling," said Tash.

She started to get changed, leaving Dani staring dreamily into space, probably still dancing her solo in her mind.

"How's Helen's part going?" Tash asked after a while.

"I don't know," Dani replied, finally looking as if she was back in the real world. "I'll get her to tell me all the details this weekend when she finally has a break from learning it!"

"Then you have to tell *us* all the details too," said Anisha. "She's so lucky. I can't wait to hear all about it."

On Saturday, Dani's parents drove down from their home in Durham to visit Dani and Helen and take them out for lunch to celebrate their dad's birthday. Tash and Anisha helped Dani decide on a pale-pink top to wear with her grey skinny jeans, and Tash lent her a pink sparkly bracelet to go with it.

Ballet Stars

Dani danced around Coppélia all morning, giddy with excitement about telling her parents everything about the show and her solo. When her mum called her on her mobile to say they'd arrived, she dashed out of the room, turning to wave to the others and almost smacking into the door because she hadn't stopped running. Tash and Anisha laughed and then watched out of the window as their friend walked off down the driveway in the sun with her sister, skipping every few steps.

Tash and Anisha spent the rest of the day outside. It was a wonderfully warm May day, and Tash knew that she'd been thinking too much about ballet and not enough about schoolwork. So they took their school books outside and had a surprisingly nice afternoon doing their maths homework together. By the time Dani came back, they had finished and were lying on the grass making a long daisy chain. They saw Dani and Helen get out of their parents' car and start walking back towards the school building.

"Dani!" Tash and Anisha shouted as loudly as they could, kneeling up and waving wildly at her. She spotted them immediately and headed their way.

"Did you have a good time?" asked Anisha, when Dani had sat down next to them.

"It was okay," said Dani with a shrug.

She picked a daisy and twirled it around in her fingers.

"Where did you go?" Tash asked.

"Just some Italian restaurant. I had pizza."

Tash felt worried. Dani didn't seem at all like herself – she was being so quiet, and she'd been in such a good mood earlier.

"Yum," said Anisha with a grin, but Dani didn't smile back. "Did Helen tell you how her role's going?" Anisha asked eagerly.

"All right, I think," said Dani.

"Well, what's it like?" asked Tash.

"I don't know!" snapped Dani. "I didn't ask for a demonstration."

Ballet Stars

Tash didn't understand Dani sometimes. If Helen was *her* sister, she'd have been desperate for all the details.

"Guess what? Mum and Dad asked if you both want to come and stay with us for half-term!" said Dani.

"That sounds great!" cried Tash. "I'll phone Mum this evening and ask her. I'm sure it'll be fine – she's going away for work that week anyway."

"I'll ask my parents too," said Anisha. "We'll have so much fun!"

"It'll be like a proper holiday," said Tash. "Even without lessons, Aurora House still feels like school when we stay here for half-term."

"Oh, I really hope your parents say yes!" said Dani. "We'll have the best time."

"You never said what your parents thought about your solo," Tash said to Dani. "Were they excited?"

"Yeah, they were pleased," replied Dani. "They were head over heels about *Helen's* part."

"Obviously!" said Tash. "She's the star of the show."

"I bet they're just as pleased about *your* solo," said Anisha. "It's a big deal to have a solo in Year Seven."

She smiled at her two friends and Tash smiled back. It was so nice of Anisha to say that, and to be so proud of her friends, even though she didn't have a solo herself. Dani still didn't look up, though.

"Yeah, sure," she mumbled. "The sun's giving me a headache. I'm going inside."

"We'll come with you," Tash said, getting up and grabbing her maths books.

Anisha stood up too and the three of them wandered back inside together. Tash and Anisha chatted about their plans for the next day, but Dani was quiet. Tash thought it must be a really bad headache to make her usually chirpy friend suddenly so silent.

"Do you want me to go and ask Dr Stevens for some headache tablets for you?" she asked.

"No, thanks," Dani replied. She gave Tash a small smile. "I'm okay really."

But Tash could tell that she wasn't. She was smiling, sure, but it wasn't a cheeky, brilliant Dani smile. It looked like she was only pretending.

Chapter 6

The next morning Dani seemed to have bounced back to her usual cheerful self, and Tash soon forgot that her friend had been weirdly quiet all evening on Saturday – there was just so much else to think about, after all. Most of it was exciting, and thoughts of half-term fun, and ballet steps, costumes and dancing onstage filled Tash's head, but soon she was forced to think about things that were less fun. Like schoolwork.

"Tash, stay behind for a minute, please," Mr Kent said at the end of Monday morning's English lesson, when the rest of the class were trooping off to their history classroom.

Tash looked worriedly at Dani and Anisha, then turned and went to Mr Kent's desk.

"I have to say, I was expecting a better story from you," Mr Kent said, pointing at Tash's myth story, which was on his desk in front of him.

Tash felt her stomach plummet.

"I tried…" she began.

"Did you?"

Mr Kent's words silenced her. She hadn't tried, not really.

"Look," said Mr Kent, "I know that ballet is the most important thing for everyone at this school, but you have four hours of dance classes a day. That's more than enough time to learn steps and rehearse for the show. When you're on school time we expect you to focus on school things. That includes your supervised homework time, and any extra hours you need to use in order to get your schoolwork done properly. Clear?"

"Yes," Tash replied in a tiny voice.

"You're good at English, Tash. You made some great points in the lesson today. Just try to get your head out of the ballet studio and focus a bit more when you do this week's homework, okay?"

"I will, I promise," said Tash, and Mr Kent smiled at her.

"Good. Now off you go to your next lesson."

Tash hurried off to history, relieved that Mr Kent hadn't been more cross with her, and promising herself over and over again that she would start trying much, much harder.

But it was a promise that was easy to forget as rehearsals for the show went on. By the end of the week, Miss Anderbel had finished teaching Tash the short Lilac Fairy solo and had taught Dani and Lily-May their solos too. Tash watched them both dancing whenever she wasn't wrapped up in practising her own steps. Lily-May was already looking near-perfect at the quick, delicate steps of her fairy solo and whenever Tash watched Dani dance, she saw a smile of such loveliness on her friend's face that it brought a smile to her own face too. Tash could see why the teachers had chosen her for the part.

"Tash, Dani and Lily-May," Miss Anderbel called at the end of the class on Friday. "From next week, I'd like you to rehearse your group dance with Juliet, Emma and Poppy instead of going to your contemporary ballet lessons on Mondays."

Tash and Dani grinned at each other. Tash liked contemporary classes and she knew that Dani loved them too, because they sometimes got to make up their own dances, but being asked to go to a special rehearsal with only a few other dancers made her feel like a grown-up ballerina.

"We'll use the small studio, so please meet me there," Miss Anderbel added.

The three girls nodded and then ran out to the

changing room to get ready for morning school.

"What was that about?" asked Anisha, who was already half changed.

"Extra rehearsals with the Year Eight fairies," explained Dani.

"Cool," said Anisha. "Do you get to miss school lessons?"

"No," sighed Tash, suddenly thinking that an extra rehearsal that got her out of maths would be even more special. "Just contemporary ballet on Mondays."

She thought about the extra rehearsals on the way to geography, which was their first lesson. After two terms of sharing a common room with them, she knew the Year Eight girls pretty well. But she'd never done ballet with them. She hoped that she didn't look rubbish compared to three girls who'd had an extra year of training, especially because she was the one who'd been chosen for the main role in their scene.

* * *

On Monday morning, Miss Anderbel had another surprise for them, and it was one that made Tash think that dancing with girls in the year above her was *nothing*. Because now they were all going to be dancing with the best dancers in the school – the graduating students.

"Most of Year Thirteen have solo parts in the wedding scene, and we want to make it look like Aurora has lots of guests at her wedding, so we've decided that all of the fairies, Lilac Fairy attendants and party guests from the first scene – that's all of you – will be guests at the wedding, too. You'll be in your fairy costumes still, and you won't have too much dancing to do except for one group dance, but you will be in the background onstage for the whole scene."

Thrills ran around the room and escaped in gasps and squeaks of joy.

"When do we learn the dance?" asked Anisha.

"I'm glad you're so keen," laughed Miss Anderbel. "You'll need to come to some of Year

Thirteen's rehearsals. Mr Watkins has asked for you all to miss your *pas de deux* class on Fridays for the next few weeks and join the rehearsals instead."

"Is Mr Watkins teaching us the dance?" asked Dani.

"Yes," replied Miss Anderbel, and Tash and her friends looked at each other anxiously. Mr Watkins was scary enough as a headteacher. Tash thought she might be too afraid to be taught a ballet dance by him – she was definitely going to get nervous and mess it all up!

"I'm sure I don't need to tell you that you'll have to work extremely hard in his rehearsals," said Miss Anderbel.

Tash nodded, her head bobbing up and down in time with the rest of the class. All of them were silent. All of them were thinking about Friday and wondering what a rehearsal with Mr Watkins and the school's best dancers would be like. It was exciting, but it was also really, really scary.

By the time they got to the science lab, the silence had disappeared and everyone was talking about one thing.

"I hope we get to watch the older girls and boys do their solos," said Anisha.

"We'll get to watch Helen dance!" Tash said, turning to Dani with excitement.

"Like I haven't seen *that* before," scoffed Dani.

She scribbled the date at the top of a page in her exercise book and began to copy the diagram Mr Jones, their science teacher, had drawn on the board. Tash was really surprised that Dani wasn't more excited. Helen was *her* sister, after all – she should be more thrilled than anyone that she'd get to dance onstage with her!

"I know, but a rehearsal is *different*," Tash insisted. "We'll get to see her learning really difficult stuff and we can see how Mr Watkins teaches her to do the steps. Aren't you interested in that?"

"I can hear the word 'rehearsal' and I can hear

the word 'dance'," said Mr Jones, calling across the sound of chatter. "It's funny, I can't hear the words 'leaves' or 'sunlight' or 'oxygen' at all, and I thought we were learning about plants, not about ballet. I can tell you right now, ballet is not going to be in your science exam at the end of term."

Tash tried to exchange an eye roll with Dani, but Dani's head was already bent over her diagram as she filled in the labels. Tash turned to Anisha instead, who was gazing at Dani with confusion in her dark-brown eyes, but the classroom had gone silent and studious, and there was no way to ask Dani what was wrong.

Tash sighed, and started copying down the diagram too. She knew she *should* be concentrating as hard as she could in lessons so that she could do well in the exams, but ballet filled her brain completely, and now she was worrying about Dani as well. There just wasn't space for science!

* * *

Whatever was bothering her, Dani seemed to have got over it by the extra rehearsal with the three Year Eight girls that afternoon. She was just as excited as Tash about learning more of their part for the show. They got changed into their ballet clothes as usual, in the big changing room that all of the students used before and after their classes. But Tash couldn't help feeling like she, Dani and Lily-May were special because they were getting their own rehearsal, just for the fairies.

She didn't want Anisha to feel left out, so she didn't keep going on about it like Lily-May, who was talking about it loudly so that everyone could hear. But she guessed that Anisha could tell just how she felt anyway.

"Have fun!" grinned Anisha, turning towards the studio for their normal contemporary ballet class. "Show those Year Eights that Year Sevens can dance just as well as them!"

Tash and Dani grinned back at her, and then at each other. They turned the opposite way and walked down the short corridor to the smallest studio, where they found Lily-May and the others all ready and waiting for them.

They started with a warm-up at the *barre* and Tash watched the older girls carefully to see if there were steps that they could do better than she could, and trying to pick up some tips.

"Tash, why are you holding your arm like that?" Miss Anderbel asked, while Tash was trying to imitate the way Poppy moved hers.

Tash looked in the mirror. Her arms didn't look like Poppy's at all – somehow trying so hard to make them look the same had made her do things wrong instead. She moved her arm back to the position that felt natural to her.

"Thank you," said Miss Anderbel.

Tash looked in the mirror again and saw that her arm movements looked just the same as Dani's and Lily-May's, almost as good as Poppy's – and definitely much better than they'd looked a few seconds ago. She gave her head a tiny shake and tried to focus only on what she was doing instead of looking at everyone else.

The rehearsal was a lot of fun. Miss Anderbel taught them the bit near the start of the scene when they would run on to the stage to the sound of tinkling music, curtsey to the King and Queen and begin to dance together. The steps were pretty and Tash saw her reflection in the mirror, smiling broadly, as she danced. Because she was the Lilac Fairy, she was usually in the middle of the stage, with Dani on one side of her and Juliet on the other.

When the two hours were up, Miss Anderbel stood back and watched them dance what they'd learned so far. They were facing the mirror at the front of the studio and Tash caught sight of the six of them in a line, standing in steady *arabesques*, arms pointing towards the corner and heads up, their legs all held at exactly the same height, and she felt a bubble of magic in her stomach. This was going to look *so* good. She couldn't wait for everyone else to see it!

Sparkling Solo

* * *

By Friday morning, everyone in Year Seven and Eight was mad with excitement – half-term was only a day away and they had their first rehearsal with the school's top students later that day. Tash was still nervous about being taught by Mr Watkins, though. What if he asked them to do something and she couldn't do it or forgot the steps? Miss Anderbel was really patient, but Mr Watkins usually only taught the senior students. They were probably always able to learn things really quickly. Tash hoped that he wasn't going to expect the same from Year Seven.

But they had their own ballet class and rehearsal to get through first. After an hour of exercises at the *barre* and in the centre, and then practising their dances for the show in their own small groups, Miss Anderbel came up with another idea.

"You've all worked so hard on your dances," she said. "And as your half-term holiday starts tomorrow, I think it's time we all got to see them properly! Let's have the Lilac Fairy attendants first."

Anisha and the others moved into their starting positions, and Tash, Dani and Lily-May sat on the floor at the front of the studio with their backs against the wall.

This was the first time Tash had seen the group dance and she loved watching her friends swirl around the room. Anisha and the others had obviously practised loads and their pretty *pas de chats* and *arabesques* were all perfectly in time with each other, even if the steps weren't quite dazzling enough for the stage yet. Miss Anderbel called out a few corrections as they danced, and every now and then she reminded them what was next, but it didn't look as if they needed reminders. It looked as if they could do the steps in their sleep already, even though the performance was still over a month away.

Tash went next, and she enjoyed every second

of performing her role for the first time. She was proud of her solo, the difficult but lovely steps that she had *almost* got just right, and it was fun to show it to her friends.

"Very nice," Miss Anderbel said at the end. "Keep working on that ending, but it's nearly there."

Tash nodded, catching her breath with her hands on her hips. She knew that her feet and her brain hadn't got the hang of the timing for the last section of the dance yet. She promised herself that she'd press it into her mind so deeply that she'd be able to do it in her sleep, too, just like Anisha and the others.

She wouldn't have a proper ballet studio to use during half-term, but she hoped she'd be able to get in a bit of practice at Dani's house. And if not, she had the music on her iPod and she could listen to it over and over and imagine herself doing the steps. She could watch videos online, too, and get the timing absolutely perfect in her head. If she managed that, maybe when she came back to school, she'd get it right with her feet, too. She sat back down next to Dani, who was twisting her hands together. Tash gave her an encouraging smile.

She turned her attention to Lily-May, who was dancing beautifully in front of her. She looked ready for the stage already – all she needed was a tutu and some lights. Tash tried really hard not to be jealous, and to remind herself that her own solo was more difficult than Lily-May's. But it was hard when Miss Anderbel cried "Perfect!" at the end. Tash wanted her teacher to think that *she* was perfect, too.

Then it was Dani's turn, and Tash stopped worrying about her own dance and focused on her friend. Dani started dancing with a smile, but it soon fell into a frown and her eyes dropped to look at the floor as she concentrated.

"Pas de bourrée right," said Miss Anderbel, starting to talk her through the steps when it was

obvious that Dani couldn't remember them. "*Pas de bourrée* left. Arms."

Tash dug her fingernails into the palms of her hands, feeling agony for her friend. Dani could do the dance, she'd seen her dance it beautifully only half an hour ago when they were practising! Tash didn't understand why she was messing it up now. Dani made more mistakes and with every wrong step she took, she looked more and more miserable.

"Eyes up," said Miss Anderbel, when Dani reached her finishing pose, but Dani barely raised her head. "Okay, well, it needs some work. But I think you just got nervous about people watching. I know you can do it better than that."

Dani nodded and sat down next to Tash.

"It's scary dancing by yourself for the first time," Tash whispered.

"What are you talking about?" muttered Dani. "You were fine."

Tash didn't know what to say to that.

"You'll be fine too, next time," she said, in the end. She crossed her fingers and hoped it was true.

Chapter 7

Tash and Anisha tried to cheer Dani up all through Friday. At lunchtime they made up silly songs to the tune of the music for her solo, and they kept talking about how much fun they were going to have in half-term, but nothing worked. Dani stayed quiet and sad, and that made Tash feel sad too.

"We've got six weeks until the show," Tash said to her while they were changing into their leotards and tights at the end of the day, ready for their rehearsal with Mr Watkins and the Year Thirteen students. "You'll know the dance really well by then."

"I *do* know it," said Dani, sighing.

She was changed and sitting on the bench, holding her soft ballet shoes in her hands, the faded pink ribbons trailing down towards the floor. "I could do it when it was just me and Miss Anderbel. Performing it in front of everyone else made me forget the steps. And that means I'm probably going to mess it up even more when I'm performing it on the City Ballet stage."

"We'll help you," promised Tash.

Anisha nodded energetically. "We'll do *anything* to get the steps to stick in your mind," she agreed.

"Thanks," replied Dani, her face brightening a little. "You two are the best!"

"Anyway," said Anisha. "Let's forget about all *that* now. We've got an important rehearsal to go to!"

"Anisha's right," said Tash. "This is going to be great!"

"Yeah," Dani replied quietly. "Fantastic."

The rehearsal wasn't as scary as Tash had thought it would be. Mr Watkins was much sterner than Miss Anderbel, but the Year Sevens were all too afraid of him to chatter or let their attention wander, so he didn't have to shout at anyone at all.

Tash felt very small standing near the older students. The girls were all dancing in pointe shoes and the boys looked so tall and strong; they all seemed very grown-up and professional. Tash knew that some of them had already got jobs for next year, dancing with real ballet companies, and the others were busy going to auditions. They were so close to the dream life – and she wanted to be just like them.

Whenever she wasn't dancing, Tash watched Helen closely and imagined what it must be like to be her, to have the starring role for the whole ballet, to know that Mr Watkins and the other teachers had chosen you out of everyone in the school. It must feel wonderful. She wondered if Helen felt nervous. Tash knew that *she* would be, if it was her, but Helen didn't seem to be worrying at all. She listened to Mr Watkins calmly and carefully and then did the steps as he asked, sometimes stopping to ask a question and then trying things out, stepping easily up onto her toes and spinning around or balancing on one foot in an *attitude* or an *arabesque en pointe*, as if it was the easiest, most natural thing in the world. Tash wished it felt like that for her.

"Okay, we'll go from the last part of the *pas de deux*," said Mr Watkins, "and then straight into the group dance. Party guests, fairies," he looked at the Year Sevens and Eights, "you kids should be standing still in your places during the *pas de deux*. Be ready to start when Helen and Tom finish."

Tash stood up straight with one foot pointed

behind her, as Mr Watkins had told them to. Dani was standing to one side of her and Anisha was on the other.

"I can't wait for you to meet my friends from home when we're there next week," Dani whispered to Tash when Helen and Tom, the Prince, had started dancing. "I've had loads of ideas for fun things we can do. This is going to be the best half-term ever!"

"Shh," Tash whispered back. "I'm watching."

She heard Dani huff out an annoyed sigh but Tash couldn't even tear her eyes away from the dancers to look at her friend. It was just a rehearsal, no tutus, no glitter, no lights, but it was magical. The *pas de deux* dance that Aurora and the Prince did together at the end of the wedding scene was in three parts. They had a long, slow duet, then a solo each, and finally a fun, fast duet with jumps and lots of *pirouettes* and some really impressive lifts. They were only doing the fast part now, and already Tash couldn't wait to see the rest.

Helen was amazing. Tash wished that she was *her* sister. She hoped that one day she'd be able to dance like that, too.

"Tash, stay behind please," Mr Kent said again at the end of the hour of supervised homework time on Friday evening.

Tash's face fell as she watched the rest of the class run off to the common room for free time before bed. She could tell from Mr Kent's expression that he was disappointed with her. She'd been *trying* to pay more attention in lessons, but with all the excitement of the extra rehearsals with the older students, maybe she hadn't been trying hard enough.

"Many of your teachers have spoken to me this week," said Mr Kent. "They've all told me the same thing: you're very bright when you actually pay attention, but you're spending at least half of every lesson daydreaming."

"I'm sorry," Tash blurted out. "It's just the

show… I really want to dance well and it's all I can think about."

"That's not good enough, Tash," Mr Kent replied and his voice was much sterner than it had been the last time he'd had to tell her off. "Everyone here wants to dance well, and they all manage to pay attention in their academic lessons too."

Tash looked down at her shoes and nodded.

"If your solo is having such a bad effect on your schoolwork, perhaps it would be best if someone else danced the Lilac Fairy."

Tash's head shot up and she looked Mr Kent directly in the eyes.

"No!" she cried. "I'll try harder, I really will. And I won't daydream, and I'll do really well in the exams, I *promise*."

There was nothing he could have said that would have made her more determined to do better at school. Having a solo in the show felt like the best thing that had ever happened to her; she *couldn't* let it be taken away from her.

"One more chance," said Mr Kent, and Tash nodded. "There are only three weeks to go until the exams. Half-term starts tomorrow. I want to see a big difference when you come back."

Tash worried that everyone in her class would wonder why she had been asked to stay behind, but in the common room, nobody could talk about anything except the rehearsal with Mr Watkins. Nobody, that is, except Dani. She was the only one who seemed completely unimpressed by the whole thing. Tash didn't understand it at all.

"But she's your sister!" she exclaimed when Dani said that she wasn't bothered about seeing the rest of the *pas de deux*.

"Big deal," said Dani. "Have you finished that maths homework?"

"No," groaned Tash, her mind turning back to schoolwork and her promise to Mr Kent. "I don't get it. I don't remember learning any of this in the lesson!"

"Let me see what you've done," said Anisha, holding out her hand for Tash's maths book.

Tash handed it over and while she was waiting for Anisha to look through her work, she clicked onto YouTube on her laptop almost automatically. There was a Lilac Fairy video Lily-May had mentioned that she'd been meaning to watch...

"You really weren't paying attention in the lesson!" said Anisha with a laugh. "Look, this should be a nine..."

Tash's head snapped up at Anisha's words – what was she *doing*? Mr Kent had given her one last chance and already her mind was drifting back to ballet. She had to focus – if she didn't work hard at school stuff, she wouldn't get to be the Lilac Fairy at all.

The Lilac Fairy was important; and now that meant maths was, too.

On Saturday morning, while they were packing their things for their stay at Dani's house, Tash and Anisha tried to help Dani with her solo. She went through it slowly with them, dancing as well as she could in the cramped space of Coppélia dorm. They'd both seen her dance it so many times that they knew most of it themselves, but to Tash's surprise, Dani didn't need any help at all remembering it.

"Eyes up, Dani!" Tash said, in a brilliant impression of Miss Anderbel.

But Dani didn't even need reminding of that. She was dancing well!

"Maybe it was just a weird one-time nervous thing," said Anisha.

"Let's test it," said Tash, as Laura and Toril came into the room. "Watch Dani dance," she said to them.

"No, Tash..." protested Dani, but Laura and Toril were already sitting down on the end of Laura's bed and waiting for Dani to start.

She began to dance. She looked at the little audience in front of her. And then she stopped.

"I've forgotten," she said.

"You can't have!" said Anisha. "You did it perfectly, like, five seconds ago."

"Start again," suggested Tash.

Dani went back to the beginning and tried to get it right. She got halfway through, not dancing as well as she had before, then she turned the wrong way, did a completely wrong step, and stopped.

"I can't do it," she said.

She dropped to the floor and put her head in her hands. Tash put an arm around her and hugged her.

"We'll help you," she whispered. "I promise."

At least they had a clue to what the problem was now – dancing by herself in front of an audience made Dani freak out and forget the steps. Tash thought back to the Christmas performance and the dance club they'd started for fun last term. Had Dani got stage fright then? Tash didn't think so. Dani always seemed like the most confident one of them all. So what was different this time?

And more importantly, how would they ever help her to overcome her fear?

Chapter 8

In their first two terms at Aurora House, Tash, Dani and Anisha had all stayed at school for the half-term week, and it had always been fun, but going to stay at Dani's house would be even better. Tash and Anisha had never been there before, not even in the Christmas or Easter holidays.

It was too far for Dani's parents to drive to Aurora House and back again in one day, so instead the three girls were travelling by train, with Helen in charge. It was exciting to be allowed to travel all the way across the country by themselves, and they spent ages in the shop at the station near school, choosing magazines and sweets for the journey.

"Let's stay up really late and watch films tonight," Dani said when they were on their way, speeding past fields dotted with lambs. She turned to sit cross-legged in her seat with her back against the window. "And then tomorrow, we could get our homework over with, or we could go shopping."

"Shopping!" said Tash and Anisha in unison, and all three of them burst out laughing.

"I'm not taking you," said Helen.

She was sitting next to the window across the aisle from Dani and Tash, with Anisha next to her and a music theory textbook open on the fold-down table – although she'd spent the whole journey so far texting her friends instead of revising for her important A-level exams.

"We don't need you to," scoffed Dani. "School rules don't count at home. Mum will let us get the bus by ourselves."

"We should do some revision this week too, though," said Anisha.

"Yeah, you're right," sighed Tash.

"Let's not think about exams!" said Dani. "We're on holiday. Let's talk about fun stuff!"

Tash and Anisha laughed. The sweets were gone before the first hour had passed, but the magazines were left unread. They spent the entire journey talking about their plans for the week and laughing about the latest school gossip.

It was quite late by the time they arrived at the train station in Durham, where Dani's dad was waiting for them. They all dumped their bags in the boot of his car and clambered in. Helen sat in the front and talked quietly with her dad while Dani pointed out everything they passed to her friends in the back of the car.

"That was my junior school...that's the

secondary school I'd have gone to if I didn't get into ballet school…"

"Speaking of ballet school," her dad interrupted. "How's this term going, Dani?"

"It's all right," Dani answered with a quick shrug. "The shopping centre is down that road there."

Tash noticed that Dani had avoided answering the question about school properly, and she wondered if it had anything to do with her problems performing her solo. She was still trying to think of a way to talk to Dani about it and find out if she was okay, when the car stopped outside a row of houses. They all got out and reclaimed their bags before going into the house.

Tash had met Dani's parents a couple of times before, at the beginning and end of terms, and Dani's mum was friendly and welcoming. The house was bright and cool inside, a lovely break after the stuffiness of the long train journey, and as soon as she stepped through the door, Tash could smell the dinner that Dani's mum had ready for them.

After giving Dani and Helen hugs, she turned to Tash and Anisha. "Why don't you girls take your things upstairs? Dinner will be ready in about five minutes."

Dani led the way up the stairs and around a corner to her bedroom. She pushed open the door, immediately dropping her bag on the floor in the middle of the small room and flopping onto her bed. Then she bounced straight back up and threw out her arms wide.

"Welcome to my room!" she cried.

Tash and Anisha put their bags down and looked around. Tash had found it impossible to imagine what Dani's bedroom would look like, because to her, Dani's room was Coppélia dorm. But Dani's bedroom at home was nothing like Coppélia. The walls were bright pink and there were photos and posters all over the place – pop stars and ballet dancers and framed photos of Dani with Helen, Dani with her parents and grandparents, Dani with some other girls her own age, and – the one Tash found herself staring at – Dani a few years younger, dressed in a pale-pink tutu with flowers crowning her blonde hair and a cheeky, happy smile on her face.

"That's from a show we did at my old dance school," said Dani.

"You look really happy," said Tash.

"Yeah," said Dani. "It was fun. Dancing onstage was just…perfect. I loved it."

Tash smiled at her, and Anisha came over to look at the picture.

"Dancing in the Aurora House show will be just as much fun," said Anisha.

Dani's face darkened. "No, it's not the same," she said. "Those shows were on a tiny stage and there weren't as many people watching as there will be at the City Ballet theatre."

"Of course, everything will be bigger and scarier at first," agreed Tash. "But dancing on that stage will be more fun and exciting than any performance we've ever done before."

"But it will also feel much, much worse when I mess my solo up in front of such a big audience," said Dani.

Tash looked at Anisha, who looked back at her with a worried expression. Neither of them knew what to say.

"Dinner!" they heard Helen call. Anisha's stomach gurgled, breaking up the gloomy mood, and they all giggled and ran down the stairs.

"Aargghh!" groaned Tash, dropping her head down onto the table where they were revising for their exams. "I don't get this!"

It was almost the end of half-term, and after days of fun, hanging around in the local shopping centre, playing board games in Dani's bedroom, practising ballet in the living room and meeting Dani's friends from junior school, they'd finally decided it was time for some schoolwork.

"What are you doing?" asked Anisha, looking up from her geography book.

Tash sat up again. "Those maths practice questions. They don't make any sense!"

She pointed down at her maths book, where she'd written numbers and rubbed them out so many times that the squared paper was now covered in grey smudges.

"Let me see," said Anisha, pulling Tash's book towards her.

While she sat frowning at what Tash had done, Tash danced her fingers across the table, trying to make them do the steps of her Lilac Fairy solo.

"This is stupid," said Tash, frustration getting the better of her. "What I *really* need to practise is ballet."

"Me too," agreed Dani, who was sitting opposite her working on history revision. "No one's going to ask me to stand up and perform the features of a castle for them."

"Let's have a ballet break," said Tash.

She pushed her chair back and stood up,

dropping her pencil onto the table. Dani did the same, but Anisha looked up at them anxiously.

"We need to revise!" she pleaded.

"Come on," Dani said, taking Anisha's pen out of her hand. "We've been studying for ages. Let's just go through our dances a couple of times, then we'll get back to revision."

"Okay." Anisha gave in. "We could get Helen to practise with us, too!"

"She's probably busy," said Dani. "Anyway, I want to rehearse without her."

"But if we have Helen, we can go through the end scene as well," said Anisha.

"I know – let's perform it all for your parents this evening," suggested Tash suddenly, and Anisha's eyes lit up, schoolwork completely forgotten.

Dani hesitated and Tash knew then that it was a good idea. Dani would surely be able to dance well in front of an audience that was just her parents. And if she could do that, she'd get some of her confidence back!

"Yeah!" said Anisha. "Come on, Dani. It's good practice."

"I thought maths was what we needed practice at," protested Dani.

"You can say the times tables while you dance," said Anisha.

"Go and ask Helen," said Tash. "We'll push the furniture out of the way."

Dani sighed and disappeared, and Tash and Anisha cleared the middle of the living room so they were left with the big wooden floor to dance on, the way they had done every morning they'd been here to do their ballet exercises. A minute later, Dani came back with Helen and all their ballet shoes.

"You guys really can't go five minutes without dancing, can you?" said Helen, but she was smiling, and Tash knew that she couldn't, either.

Later, Tash sat on the arm of the sofa and watched Helen dancing her solo from the final scene. It was pretty and delicate with lots of light steps and quick turns. Even though Helen had complained that they'd dragged her away from the TV show she was watching in her room, as soon as she started dancing she was totally serious. She looked as if she was really onstage in front of hundreds of adoring fans, instead of in a living room with just the three girls, and two cats who were ignoring her completely. She was only dancing in flat shoes instead of *en pointe*, and every now and then she had to dodge an obstacle like a sofa or a bookcase, but she was still amazing.

They made a playlist of tracks from *The Sleeping Beauty* on Dani's laptop; they were only going to perform a few bits – their solos, Anisha's group dance, and the dance from the end of the ballet – but they wanted them all to flow on from each other like a proper performance instead of having to mess about finding the right music in between each dance.

When Dani's parents got home from work, the

girls made them sit down in the living room. They'd all changed into ballet leotards and tights, and had put their hair up into proper ballet buns, too. They wanted to look like dancers onstage, even if it was only in Dani's living room.

They started with the fairy group dance from the first scene, slow and grand, and full of *arabesques* and *pirouettes*. Tash and Dani danced it really well together, and Tash couldn't help grinning to herself. There was no trace of nerves in Dani's performance – perhaps Tash's idea really would help Dani overcome her fear.

Anisha's group dance was next, although as she was the only one there it automatically became a solo. Tash watched her, and wished her friend had been given a solo part. She was such a natural performer – even though it was only for an audience of two people, she looked as if she was having a great time.

Then it was Dani's turn. She walked out into the middle of the room like a perfect ballerina and stood in her starting position. The music began, and so did she. Tash watched her in agony. She was desperate for Dani to get this right, because she was sure that if she could do the dance now, in front of her parents, it would help her to feel better about performing the same solo for a proper audience.

To Tash's delight, Dani danced beautifully. She was coming to the end and everything had gone well so far. As she turned to her left for a final set of *developpés*, unfolding her leg to the side as high as she could, Tash saw her look at Helen, who was watching from the corner. Dani faltered a little, wobbled out of the *developpé* and missed the next one out entirely, but she covered it well and kept smiling. When Dani finished dancing, her parents clapped a lot and she beamed at them, her smile brightening up her whole body. She stepped to the side of the room and let Tash take centre stage.

Tash performed her dance better than she ever had before, even though she had to make all her movements smaller so that she didn't go crashing into a wall or a sofa. She spun around in *pirouettes* and leaped through small *sissonne*s as if they were what she had been born to do. Her solo seemed to speed by and before she knew it she was at the end and it had gone brilliantly.

Dani's parents clapped again and Tash realized then that it had been her first performance of the solo for an audience that wasn't just the rest of her class. It felt great and she couldn't wait to do it again. Her heart raced as she remembered that the next time would be on the City Ballet stage in front of a much bigger audience – all her teachers, the other parents, important people from the City Ballet Company and, most importantly to Tash, Mum.

She caught her breath while watching Helen dance – it was magical. Dani's parents clapped louder and longer for her than they had for any of the other performances. It made sense to Tash; Helen was the best dancer, after all, and her dance was far more difficult than anyone else's. But as she glanced at Dani she saw disappointment on her face.

No one made any mistakes in the final group dance, but Tash kept catching sight of Dani – and her bright cheerfulness seemed to fade with every step she danced.

"I don't know how you're able to get your leg that high," Dani's mum said to Helen while they were eating dinner, after all four of them had changed back into normal clothes and put the furniture back where it was meant to be.

"It's amazing," agreed Dani's dad. "Your whole dance was just fantastic."

"It must be even harder in pointe shoes!" said Dani's mum.

"Yeah," said Helen. "Well, we practise a lot."

"We're counting the days until we can see you dance onstage," said Dani's mum. "The main role!"

"Our star!" said Dani's dad.

"Your only one," muttered Dani.

"What was that?" asked her dad.

"Oh, I'm amazed you remember I'm even here," said Dani.

"Dani…" warned her mum. "I hope you're not jealous. Your sister's worked very hard for a very long time to get this far. You'll have your chance."

"As if I'd be jealous of *her*," said Dani, her voice rising in anger.

Tash looked down at her plate, feeling awkward.

"What's your problem?" demanded Helen, glaring at Dani. "You've been in a mood all afternoon."

"*You're* my problem!" Dani shot back across the table. She did a high-pitched, horrible impression of her sister: "'Oh, I'm Helen and I'm a *perfect* dancer and a *perfect* daughter and I'm everybody's *favourite*.' I can't wait to go back to school so I don't have to see you so much any more."

She slammed her fork down on the table and

scraped her chair back across the tiled kitchen floor, making Tash wince.

"Nobody's our favourite," said Dani's mum gently. "We love you just as much as Helen and we're just as excited about watching you perform your solo."

"Well, it doesn't feel like it," said Dani, and then she was gone.

Dani's mum looked upset and she got half out of her chair.

"Danielle!" her dad shouted. "Come back here and apologize!"

They heard Dani stomping up the stairs. Tash and Anisha looked at each other. This was awful! People had arguments at school sometimes, but seeing someone argue with their parents in their own house was different, and so much worse.

"We'll talk to her," said Tash, getting up.

She couldn't sit there for a second longer. She didn't have any brothers or sisters so she had no idea what it was like to fall out with them, and she couldn't imagine how it would feel to have to share Mum with someone else. She'd spent lots of this term envying Dani for having an amazing older sister; she hadn't realized there was another side to it – or how upsetting it might be if your sister sometimes felt like your competition.

"Hey," Tash said quietly.

She and Anisha pushed open the bedroom door Dani had slammed (twice) a minute ago. Dani was curled on her side on her bed. Tash and Anisha sat on the end of the bed and waited. Dani sniffed loudly, then sat up. Her face was streaked with messy tears.

"Do you think I'm horrible for yelling at my parents like that?" she asked.

"No," said Anisha.

"They don't think you're horrible either," said Tash.

"I bet Helen does," said Dani glumly. "Ugh, I'm going to have to say *sorry* to her." She pulled her knees up to her chest and held on to her feet. "It's not fair! They only care about watching her dance. Not me."

"I don't think that's true," said Anisha. "I used to feel like my parents were only interested in watching my little brothers play football, and they didn't care about ballet at all, but then I found out my brothers thought they preferred watching me dance and found football boring! We were both wrong. Maybe Helen thinks they're only interested in watching you."

Dani snorted. "Not likely. Did you *hear* them at dinner?"

"Your mum did say they were just as excited about your solo," said Tash, trying to find a way to make Dani feel better. "I'm sure when they come to watch the performance they'll be equally proud of both of you."

Dani didn't look so sure. "If they notice I'm there at all."

* * *

The train journey back to Aurora House was not as much fun as the one taking them away from school had been. Dani had said sorry to Helen, but everyone could tell that she was still annoyed. Helen said she'd forgiven Dani for being nasty, but it was obvious to Tash that she was still upset, too.

They had to travel together, but Helen sat in the row in front of them on the train this time, and she listened to music the whole time, texting her friends and revising for her exams and only speaking to Dani when she absolutely had to. That seemed to be fine with Dani, who didn't speak to her much either, but Tash felt awkward and sad about it all. She liked Helen a lot and looked up to her, but now she felt as if she'd have to pretend not to be interested in watching her dance. She wished she could sort it all out and help Dani to make up with her sister and feel happy again.

Dani was almost as silent as Helen. She got out her copy of *Goodnight Mister Tom* and started reading it again from the beginning. Anisha was doing geography revision next to her. Tash reluctantly got out her maths book and tried the practice questions again. She wished she hadn't spent quite so much time practising ballet and having fun during the week off, and a little bit more time getting ready for the exams. They were only two weeks away now and she still had a lot to learn.

"You were right, Anisha," she sighed. "We should have done more revision."

"It's hard when ballet is so much more fun," said Anisha.

"I'm just not any good at concentrating on schoolwork," said Tash.

"I bet you've learned more than you think," said Anisha. "We never did that practice maths test that Miss Hewett gave us. Let's try it now. That will help you see that you do remember what you need to know."

Dani and Tash agreed and they all got out the paper booklet their teacher had given them in the last lesson before half-term in case they wanted some extra practice. Tash wondered if anyone in the class had done the test, or if everyone else had spent the whole of half-term practising for the show, too.

They were all quiet for the next half-hour, working through the questions while the train sped them back to school. Tash kept looking up at Dani and Anisha, wondering if they were only pretending to be able to answer all of them. She definitely couldn't. She chewed the end of her pen worriedly. There were some questions that she could do, and a few that she could take a guess at. But on most of them, she was lost.

Anisha's phone beeped, telling them that time was up.

"I have the answer sheet here somewhere," said Anisha, pulling everything out of her bag onto her lap. "Found it!" She held a crumpled piece of paper up and grinned. "Okay, I'll call them out, and you guys mark your own. No cheating!"

Tash put cross after cross next to her answers. There was a tick every now and then, but not many. Not enough to pass.

"30 out of 40," said Anisha when they'd finished. "That's good enough."

Dani had put her pen down and gone back to staring gloomily out of the window, but Tash leaned over and saw that she'd got 32. Tash looked back at the mark she'd circled at the top of her own test.

13. She was going to fail.

Her solo would be taken from her. Even worse, what if she lost her scholarship? Then she'd have to leave Aurora House and go back to a normal school without Dani and Anisha and ballet every day, and she wouldn't *ever* have a chance to dance on the City Ballet stage.

Tears dripped over her eyelashes and started to slide down her face. She sniffed and wiped them away; she did *not* want to cry on a train. But she couldn't help it, and the more tears she wiped away, the more stung her eyes before falling onto her cheeks.

"Tash, what's wrong?" gasped Anisha.

Tash held up the maths test and showed her.

"I'm going to fail!" she cried.

"No!" said Dani coming to life again and turning to face her. She hugged Tash tightly. "We won't let that happen."

"It's too late," said Tash, hugging Dani back as hard as she could. "I should have paid more attention in lessons, and now I'm going to fail."

"You're *not*," insisted Anisha. Tash pulled away from Dani and looked at her. "We'll help you."

"But how?" asked Tash.

"Will it help if we all revise the same subjects together?" asked Dani. "We could make a revision timetable for the next two weeks. We could do a different subject every evening and we can help each other with the bits we get stuck on."

"Good idea!" said Anisha. "If we pick a time to focus on school, then we won't get distracted by ballet because we know that's revision time and we *have* to do it."

"Okay," Tash agreed. "Let's try it."

She hated the thought of giving up time that she could have spent perfecting the Lilac Fairy, but she knew her friends were right. If she didn't pass the exams, she might have to leave Aurora House and she hated that thought even more.

Chapter 9

That night, Tash lay awake worrying. She'd been running through some of her school lessons in her mind to see how much she remembered, but however hard she tried to think about history or French or science, after a few minutes her brain automatically flipped back to ballet. Even though Dani and Anisha had offered to help her, she was still panicking. She turned back and forth in her bed, trying to force herself to fall asleep.

"Are you okay, Tash?" she heard Dani whisper from the bed next to hers.

"Can't sleep," Tash whispered back.

"Exams?"

"Yeah. Can I come over?"

"Of course," Dani murmured.

She shifted over in her bed to make room, and Tash tiptoed the few steps across the floor and got under the covers. Dani pulled the duvet up over their heads so they were hidden in a cosy tent.

"I'm scared," Tash admitted.

"What about?"

"What if I do really badly in the exams and have to leave?"

"Tash, that won't happen!" Dani tried to reassure her. "We've got a plan, remember?"

"But what if the plan doesn't work?" said Tash. "I can't make myself focus. All I can think about is ballet. Even when I try not to, I can't help daydreaming about the show."

Dani was silent for a moment. "Maybe...I don't

know…how about if you try to notice when you're doing it? Every time you catch yourself thinking about ballet, you could imagine a big sign saying 'NO!' or a stop sign or something."

"Like a pair of ballet shoes with a big cross through them," giggled Tash.

"Yeah. Or Mr Kent's face when he tells us 'No ballet talk allowed'."

"That could work," said Tash. "Hear that, brain? No ballet talk allowed during exams!"

"I think you'll be fine," said Dani, squeezing her hand.

Tash finally felt herself getting sleepy. She was feeling better about everything already. She had a plan. Now she just needed one for Dani.

"I think you'll be fine, too," she said. She gave Dani a hug and then went back to her own bed.

She hoped they were both right.

On Monday evening, Tash, Dani and Anisha put their revision plan into action properly. After dinner they had supervised homework time in their form room, which was supposed to be silent.

"That doesn't have to stop us revising together," said Dani. "Let's all revise the same thing and then test each other on it afterwards."

"Good plan," said Tash. "Now I definitely can't daydream while we're meant to be working – because you'll know!"

"And you'll know if either of us spends the whole time thinking about ballet too."

"How about history today?" suggested Tash. "I feel like I've hardly done any history revision at all."

It was hard to focus on schoolwork when all she wanted to do was dance, but once Tash forced herself to put ballet out of her mind, she was surprised by how fast the supervised homework time went, and how much she managed to learn. When they tested each other in the common room afterwards, she did almost as well as Dani and Anisha.

They did geography the next day, and maths the day after that, and as the week went on, Tash started to feel better. Maybe it wasn't too late after all. Filled with new confidence and determination, she vowed to work harder than ever over the next ten days. After that, it would all come down to the questions in the exams.

Tash tapped her pen nervously on the edge of the table, waiting until Mr Kent told them they could turn over the paper with the questions for their English exam. This was the first one and she was dreading it. What if imagining a stop sign like Dani had suggested didn't work and she spent the whole hour thinking about the steps of her Lilac Fairy solo? She tried it out, painting a big red sign in her mind with the word STOP! across it. Focusing on that made her fear go away a bit, and she started to feel better.

"You can start," said Mr Kent.

He turned to the whiteboard and wrote 10:00 as

the start time and 11:00 as the finish time. Tash turned over the paper and looked at it. She felt too nervous to read the questions. They could be ones that she didn't know how to answer! She looked back up at Dani, who was sitting opposite her at the other end of their table. There weren't enough tables for everyone to have one each, so most people were sharing, sitting at the ends so that they couldn't see each other's answers.

Dani was biting her pen as she read the questions. Then she looked up and smiled at Tash. She flicked her eyes down towards the questions and then nodded slightly at Tash with another smile. Tash let her tense shoulders drop. Dani must mean that the questions were okay. She risked a glance down at them herself and saw that her friend was right. They weren't impossible at all! She could already think of how to start her first answer.

By the time she'd finished answering a question about *Goodnight Mister Tom*, it was 10:35. Twenty-five minutes for the rest of the exam, which asked her to read a newspaper article and then answer some short questions about it. She got started, but the word *lilac* in the article made her mind leap to an image of herself in a beautiful lilac tutu, and then her brain was racing through the steps of her solo and it was difficult to stop her feet from dancing them under the table.

No, she thought. *Exam. Focus.*

But her mind was still on the stage. She pictured a stop sign and then Mr Kent, and then she imagined Dani standing in front of her with arms folded, shaking her head and telling her to stop. She couldn't help smiling at the funny image of Dani with a strict-teacher expression on her face. She focused on the exam paper and carried on working.

When she finished, she saw that she had two minutes to read through what she'd written. She skimmed through her answers and felt relieved – she didn't think they were *too* bad.

"How did it go?" Dani asked, after the exam had finished.

"I did it," said Tash, grinning at her friend. "It worked!"

"Yay!" cried Dani, then clapped a hand over her mouth. They were supposed to be quiet until they got outside because other students were still doing exams.

As soon as they were out in the bright sunshine, Dani jumped on Tash, hugging her with glee.

"Thanks for your help," Tash said.

"If you want to go over that maths stuff again, we can do it at lunchtime," Anisha offered.

"Thanks," said Tash. "You guys are the best."

"Well, what else are we going to do?" asked Dani. "You're our best friend. We're not going to let you *leave*."

Tash hugged them both – she felt way more confident now than she had before, and it was all because of her friends. She was so lucky to have them. The three of them would stick together through anything – they were like sisters!

Even though it felt like exam week would never end, Friday afternoon came and at last Tash felt as if she could relax a bit. None of the exams had been as impossible as she'd feared – even maths hadn't been too bad. And the end of Friday also meant a rehearsal with the older students for the final scene of the show.

"I wish we could just rehearse in our own classes," grumbled Dani when they were getting changed.

She was still ignoring Helen as much as she could, which made the rehearsals with Year Thirteen less fun than they'd been before half-term.

"That would never work!" said Tash. "Our class and Year Eight and the Year Thirteens are all doing this scene together. We'd never be able to practise it properly if we rehearsed separately."

"I know," said Dani. "But it's so annoying

having to wait around and watch while everyone else dances and we just have to stand there with our arms in the air for ever and ever."

"My arm always aches halfway through," agreed Anisha. "I know it's meant to look grand and beautiful but it won't if we all have drooping arms by the end."

"We'll all be propping each other up," Tash giggled.

"Well, it is *The Sleeping Beauty*," added Anisha, and she pretended to fall asleep on Tash, standing up, with her feet and arms still in a ballet pose.

"Let's get this over with," said Dani, ignoring their laughter as she headed towards the studio.

Tash and Anisha followed her, but they didn't get very far before they bumped into Helen, who was coming from another studio where she'd been rehearsing.

"Dani," she said, catching her sister by the arm. "Can I talk to you for a minute? I just wanted to say—"

Dani twisted her arm out of Helen's hand and interrupted her.

"Not now," she said, without even looking Helen in the eye. "We'll be late for the rehearsal."

Dani walked off, and Helen stared after her with a worried expression. Tash sighed and looked at Anisha, who looked sadly back at her. Tash followed Dani into the studio and found a space to warm up at the *barre*, wishing she could make things right between the two sisters.

It was a slow rehearsal. After half an hour the Year Sevens still hadn't done any real dancing, and even Tash was starting to get a bit bored.

"Take a break, everyone," said Mr Watkins. "Helen, let's go through your solo again. I'm not happy with the spacing."

While Mr Watkins and Helen carried on working, Tash and the others went to the corner of the studio where they'd left their bottles of water.

"This is so boring," said Dani. "I want to dance!"

"Let's go through our solos," suggested Tash. "We've got a bit of space here, and no one's watching."

"Okay," agreed Dani.

Tash, Dani and Anisha all started to dance, but there wasn't enough room in their little corner and it wasn't long before Tash and Anisha bumped into each other. They laughed, and stopped dancing, but Dani carried on. She seemed to be completely lost in her own world – she hadn't even noticed that a few of the older students were watching, too. Then she looked up, and saw that she had an audience, and her face flushed bright red. She got her arms mixed up and did one of the steps on the wrong foot. Then she stopped.

"Carry on!" said Anisha. "That was going really well."

"I can't!" said Dani and she hurried into the corner and sat down on the floor, wrapping her arms around her legs and making herself as small as possible.

Tash and Anisha went and sat with her.

"That was so embarrassing," groaned Dani.

"Hardly anyone was watching," Tash said, in the most reassuring voice she could manage.

But Dani wouldn't get up again until Mr Watkins called them all back together to carry on with the rehearsal.

They had almost finished for the day when Mr Watkins said that, as the boy and girl from Year Thirteen who were dancing the White Cat and Puss In Boots *pas de deux* were still in an exam, they'd skip over that bit and move on to the next dance.

"We'll do it!" said a voice.

Tom, Helen's partner, got up from the floor where he'd been sitting while he and Helen were "offstage". He grabbed her hand and she got up too, and they jumped into the middle of the room.

"Okay then," said Mr Watkins, with an amused smile. "Off you go."

Tom whispered in Helen's ear and she nodded

and laughed. They must have seen the funny duet so many times in rehearsals that they both knew it off by heart. But once they started dancing, Tash and the others got a surprise: Helen and Tom had swapped roles, so that Helen was dancing the boy's part and Tom the girl's. It was meant to be a funny dance anyway, but watching Tom pretending to dance *en pointe* and be a girl cat, while Helen pretended to be Puss In Boots made it even funnier.

They exaggerated all the cat-like steps and movements and tried to pull cat-like faces, making fun of the dance while still somehow doing the steps properly. The whole room was full of laughter; even Mr Watkins was finding it funny. And then Helen tried to lift Tom up and couldn't, and Tash laughed until her stomach ached, and she fell against Anisha, who was finding it just as hilarious. When the dance finished, everyone burst into applause. Tash looked around at everyone sharing the same joke and she felt like she was part of the most wonderful school in the world.

But not everyone agreed. Not clapping, not laughing, leaning against the wall with a face like someone who'd just been told they'd never dance again, was Dani. And she was glaring at Helen as if she *hated* her.

Chapter 10

Tash tried hard not to talk about Helen in front of Dani, but she couldn't stop everyone else from doing it. In the common room and the classroom, at the dining room tables at lunchtime and in Coppélia at night, the others talked and talked about how great Dani's sister was and how much they wanted to be like her.

"I wonder what Helen's costume will be like," said Laura on Saturday evening when they were getting ready for bed. "Dani, do you know?"

"She'll have more than one, I think," said Donna.

"Beautiful tutus, I bet!" said Toril. "She's so lucky to be the star!"

Dani just shrugged and didn't say anything, and Tash could see that she felt hurt. Ever since the row at Dani's house, Tash was starting to realize what the constant praise must feel like for Dani, and she felt bad that she'd been doing the same thing until now.

"I wonder when we'll get to try on *our* costumes," said Tash, picking the one thing to talk about that she knew would make everyone forget about Helen. It worked, and they all spent the rest of the time until lights out excitedly wondering about the tutus they'd get to wear.

"Dani, why don't you try and talk to Helen?" Tash suggested on Sunday evening when the three of them were alone in their dorm.

"She's tried to talk to you," said Anisha. "She obviously wants to make up."

"Maybe she could even help you to stop being afraid of the performance," said Tash. "She's done loads of shows, I bet she's learned how to get over stage fright."

"It's not that easy," said Dani. "You don't understand."

"Can you talk to us about it, then?" Tash asked gently.

"You won't get it," insisted Dani. "You don't know what it's like to have a sister who's a million times better at ballet than you!"

"That's not true, Dani!" said Anisha. "It's just that Helen's older."

"She's been training for much longer," added Tash. "That doesn't mean that she's more talented than you."

"But that's what people see," said Dani. "Everyone knows I'm her little sister. When they watch me dance, they'll just compare me to Helen and think that I'm not as good."

Dani got up and left the room before Tash or Anisha had a chance to say anything to comfort her. Tash suddenly felt really sad for Dani, and she finally understood why she'd been so weird about the show and why she didn't want Helen's help getting over her fear.

Dani wouldn't talk to Helen, and she wouldn't talk to her friends. Tash didn't know what to do.

Miss Anderbel must have known how exhausted her Year Seven class would be after exam week, so their ballet class on Monday morning was relaxed and calm.

"You can work on your solos and group dances by yourselves today," she said. "I'm here to help anyone who needs it, and I'll be coming around to see how each of you is getting on. And while we're doing that, you'll all be taken out one at a time to try on your costumes!"

The whole class whooped with delight. Tash grinned at Dani and Anisha, and they smiled back at her just as happily.

Tash tried hard to focus on her solo, but she couldn't stop thinking about what her costume might be like and she'd only managed one proper run-through of her solo when Miss Anderbel told her it was her turn. She skipped out of the studio and ran up the stairs.

The whole upper floor of the studio block was taken up by a big costume storeroom full of tutus, dresses, leotards and other costumes that the students wore in performances. Some of the costumes were quite old and had been worn by students who were now dancers with City Ballet and other companies. Miss Anderbel had brought the *Nutcracker* costumes for their Christmas performance down to the studio, so Tash had never been in the storeroom before.

The room was packed with colour and sparkle. She wanted to reach out and run her hands along a rack filled with soft green and blue chiffon dresses, but she was afraid that she'd get in trouble for touching precious costumes. A doorway in one wall led to a small room with a desk and a sewing machine and a big mirror. Tash knocked quietly on the open door.

"Hello!" said the woman sitting at the desk. "I'm Mrs Casey."

"I'm Tash. Um, I mean, Natasha Marks."

Mrs Casey ran her finger down a list on the desk.

"Ah, our youngest Lilac Fairy. Lovely. Wait here." She disappeared into the main room and returned a moment later holding a tutu.

Tash stared at it. Did she *really* get to wear this? To dance onstage in it? It was the most beautiful thing she'd ever seen!

The leotard part was pale lilac with small flowers in the same colour along the top and around the waist, where the skirt was attached. The tutu skirt was made of loads of layers of net, dark purple and light purple and white, with a layer of thin material over the top that was shimmery and dotted with more flowers.

Seeing the look on Tash's face, Mrs Casey smiled. "Lucky you," she said.

Tash stepped forward and touched the edge of the skirt, which sparkled with a dusting of silver glitter.

"Try it on," said Mrs Casey, handing the tutu over.

Tash took it and walked over to the little curtained-off cubicle that was set up as a tiny changing room.

When she came out again, she was still gazing down at the tutu, resting her hands gently on the skirt part. She couldn't believe that she was wearing it. She looked up and saw herself reflected in the mirror. She started and walked closer. That was *her*! She looked one hundred per cent like a ballerina. Her hair was up in a bun for class and she was still wearing her soft ballet shoes. She brought her arms up above her head and moved them through some other classical ballet positions, watching her reflection the whole time, still not really believing that it was herself she saw.

"You look beautiful," said Mrs Casey. "A real star. Let me just look at those leotard straps though. We don't want anything falling down onstage!"

Tash grinned at her, and Mrs Casey got on with her work, fiddling about with pins and writing down a few notes on her list.

When she'd finished and Tash had changed back into her school leotard, she went back to her class in a daze. Now that she'd worn her costume for the first time and knew what she'd look like when she stepped onto the City Ballet stage, her daydreams were complete. And her determination to be just like dancers who had been the Lilac Fairy before her rose even higher. Mrs Casey had said she looked like a star. Now she had to dance like one, too.

* * *

With the exams out of the way, and not *too* much dread in her mind about the results, there was nothing to stop Tash watching Lilac Fairy videos on her laptop in every free moment she got. She watched them in the common room with headphones plugged in so that she didn't annoy other people watching TV or reading or watching videos on their own laptops. Sometimes she set her laptop up on the end of her bed in Coppélia and danced along with the ballerinas, imagining that she *was* them, and trying to imitate them perfectly.

"Why are you moving your hands like *that*?" Dani asked, one day, coming into their dorm while Tash was practising.

"That's how Miss Anderbel does it in this video," said Tash. Dani looked at the screen.

"Oh, okay," she replied, but she sounded unsure. "I think it looked better before. It doesn't really look like you."

"I'm not trying to dance like me," said Tash.

"I'm trying to be the Lilac Fairy. Like Miss Anderbel was. I want to be just like her."

When Tash wasn't practising her own solo, she was desperately trying to think of a way to help Dani with hers. She felt completely helpless every time she saw her friend forget the steps when anyone was watching her dance. The worst thing was that Dani could do the solo perfectly when it was only Tash and Anisha or Miss Anderbel watching. But as soon as any more people started paying attention, she lost what she was doing and crumbled.

Tash knew that the problem wasn't that the steps were too difficult or that Dani's memory was bad, but the fear of performing in front of people and being compared to Helen. Knowing that didn't seem to solve anything, though; she still couldn't think of a way to help Dani get over her stage fright.

Even Miss Anderbel didn't seem to be able to sort the problem out. After Dani performed her solo particularly badly one afternoon, Miss Anderbel took her aside to give her some advice.

"She told me all this stuff about trying to forget that the audience is there," Dani said to Tash and Anisha later. "But that doesn't help! If I could just forget anyone was watching me, it would be easy. But I *can't*. And the performance is only two weeks away!"

Tash wished she had some magic words to make everything better. But she didn't – all she could do was hug Dani and let her know that she was there for her.

Time sped by without a solution. Tash and Anisha tried to tell Dani that she *was* a good dancer, but every time they started a conversation about Helen or stage fright, Dani refused to listen and changed the subject. It was as if she was too scared to even think about it, and Tash didn't want to make her angry. The last thing they all needed was to fall out with each other.

The day of the first dress rehearsal at the grand City Ballet theatre arrived, and Tash was really nervous. She was excited about standing on the stage in her costume, but she was worried about dancing by herself with the whole school watching, and she knew that Dani must be dreading it.

They went to the theatre in coaches. The Year Seven and Eight coach was a riot of nervous noise and excited laughter, but Dani was quiet, and next to her, Tash sat silently too. Mr Kent was going to the theatre with them to help chaperone the boys and he sat down in front of Tash and Dani.

"This is all very exciting, isn't it?" he said.

"And nerve-wracking!" replied Tash.

"I'm sure you'll be fine," said Mr Kent. "You spent enough time practising and daydreaming, after all."

Tash felt her face turning red and she looked worriedly at Mr Kent until his face broke into a smile and she realized he was just teasing her.

"I'm glad to see that you got down to schoolwork properly in the end, though," he added. "I've just got the last of the exam results from your other teachers. The reports will be posted out to you in the summer holidays, but you have no need to worry, Tash. You've done quite well. You too, Dani."

Tash smiled at Mr Kent and felt relief fill her mind. She could stay at Aurora House! All that revision and the help from her amazing friends had paid off!

Dani smiled slightly at Mr Kent, too, but the relief of exam results didn't seem to be enough to shake away her worries about the performance. And that made Tash's relief fade away too. She *had* to think of something to help Dani. But the dress rehearsal was only an hour away, and the real performance was the next evening. Was it too late? Was there nothing at all that could save Dani from stage fright now?

Walking through the stage door into the theatre

was enough to distract Tash from her worries for a while. Only two terms ago she'd gone in through the audience door with a ticket to a ballet in her hand, and now she was going in as a dancer! Miss Anderbel led them through a maze of corridors, all painted pale grey, with noticeboards here and there listing performances and castings and big signs telling them to be silent because they were near the stage. They went up and up, round and round grey-painted staircases, until finally Miss Anderbel pushed open a door to a big changing room.

"Year Seven and Eight girls," she said, and they filed in, staring all around them.

Their costumes had already been brought to the theatre and were hanging on a clothes rail by the door, the tutus all upside down so that the skirts wouldn't become droopy. A sign on the door told Tash that the dressing room was usually home to the young women in the City Ballet *corps de ballet*, the most junior dancers in the company, who danced in the background of every single performance. The walls were lined with mirrors with light bulbs along the tops of them, just like in films. Underneath these, a long table ran along each wall, with chairs set out so that the dancers could sit there to do their make-up. The edges of the mirrors were covered with cards and photos: pictures of the dancers having fun backstage in costume, or on holiday, or out celebrating someone's birthday.

Tash peeked at the writing in one of the cards, and it wished a dancer called Amy good luck in a solo role. The Aurora House girls had the dressing room for that day and the next one, so the City Ballet dancers had cleared away most of their things, but it was fun to see the cards and photos and to imagine that this was where they spent every day of their lives, getting ready to dance on the stage that Tash would soon be dancing on herself. She felt a thrill run through her, tingling all the way down to her feet. She wanted her life to be just like this.

Ballet Stars

* * *

The music sounded different. It was louder and richer, and more full of joy and grace and sparkle – everything that Tash loved about ballet. It boomed out from the theatre's speakers and filled the stage and the auditorium.

From her place in the wings, Tash could see people already onstage: Chris the King, Sarah the Queen and the Year Eights who were playing party guests. The lights were bright but every now and then they dimmed and changed colour as the technicians worked out what would look best.

Tash heard the familiar twinkling music of the fairies' entrance and felt a flutter of nervousness inside her. But she put on a pretend bright smile so that no one would see how anxious she felt, and ran out onto the stage behind Dani, Lily-May and the other fairies, with Anisha right behind her, followed by the rest of their class. She watched her tutu sparkle and shine under the lights, and her smile became real.

Sparkling Solo

"Eyes up, Dani," Miss Anderbel said within five seconds, and then again a minute later.

Tash couldn't watch Dani much while she was dancing herself, but no one had stopped the music to make them start again, so she guessed that Dani was doing okay and not getting anything wrong, even if she was looking down at the floor the whole time.

When they'd finished the group fairy dance, Miss Anderbel stopped the music so that they could go through each of their solos without it the first time, to get the spacing right on the big stage.

Tash watched Dani dancing her solo from her place in the wings. Dani's tutu was pale green and yellow, and covered in flowers, with a trail of leaves snaking down the leotard and across the front of the skirt. She looked really pretty, and she was managing to get the steps right, but she still wasn't smiling and Miss Anderbel kept having to remind her not to look down at the stage.

"Dani, I've told you this a thousand times!"

the teacher cried. "Look out at the *audience*."

Dani nodded, but her head drooped even further in shame at being told off.

"Let's try it with the music," said Miss Anderbel with a sigh.

Tash watched anxiously from the darkness as her friend's costume sparkled under the light. The music started, blaring loud, and Dani began to dance. She was really trying to look up, Tash could see that. But the auditorium lights were on and even from the wings, Tash could see the faces of the older students watching from the front few rows of seats. She knew it was scary to be out on the stage, dancing in front of them, wondering if they were looking at you and thinking you were rubbish. No wonder Dani didn't feel confident, especially as she thought that the rest of the school would be comparing her to Helen.

Still, her dance was going quite well – she was a little wobbly in some of her movements, but at least she hadn't forgotten anything. Tash was feeling hopeful that Dani could pull it all together in time for the performance tomorrow as she watched her finish a step in the front left-hand corner of the stage and look out towards the audience with her chin raised. Tash saw Helen lean forward in her seat, and Dani obviously saw it too, because she stopped dancing. She was still standing in a ballet-pose, one arm stretched out high in front of her, one foot pointed behind, but she'd been standing there way too long. She faltered and looked round for Miss Anderbel, standing at the front of the auditorium.

"I'm sorry," she said quietly.

"Carry on," said Miss Anderbel. "You should be over there now."

Dani picked up the rest of the dance with a little help from Miss Anderbel, but she didn't lift her eyes from the floor again. When she finished, she ran off, disappearing into the darkness on the opposite side of the stage from where Tash was standing.

Tash watched her go with a feeling of despair. She couldn't go after her because her own solo was coming up in a few minutes. She didn't have time to go all the way around the back of the stage and find Dani, wherever she had gone. She couldn't see Anisha, so she held on to a small hope that she had been able to hurry away and comfort Dani. Tash knew that her friend would need it. Miss Anderbel looked worried, too, but Poppy was already on the stage to go through her solo, so after a second's hesitation the teacher focused back on Poppy and continued the rehearsal.

When Tash's turn came, she tried really hard to push all her worries and fears out of her mind and throw herself totally into her role. As she danced, she thought about all the tiny little details other dancers had done before her and tried to copy them. But she couldn't forget that she was dancing in a famous theatre, on the stage where her favourite dancers had performed. What if everyone in the audience the next day thought she wasn't good enough to be dancing the Lilac Fairy on the City Ballet stage? It suddenly felt like a lot of pressure.

She was desperate to dance as well as those dancers, but she'd watched so many different videos, and they were all starting to blur together in her mind. There was the way Lily-May had said she should hold her arms, and then there was a different style of movement that Miss Anderbel had done with her hands in the video, and the way she had seen Poppy dancing in rehearsals, and…and…

"Tash, what on earth are you doing with your fingers?" Miss Anderbel asked when she was halfway through her rehearsal without the music.

Tash realized that she was switching between the different versions she'd tried in the middle of her dance. She looked at her hands and her fingers looked like wilting flowers, not at all the way she'd wanted them to.

Tash stopped dancing, and looked worriedly

at the rows of students watching her. She went to the front of the stage so that she could speak quietly to Miss Anderbel.

"Sorry, I got a bit…a bit confused," she said. "I was trying to copy the way you danced in a video I found online."

She suddenly felt silly and embarrassed because everyone was watching. Maybe they all imagined that she thought she was as good as Miss Anderbel.

"I wanted to be like the other dancers I watched, too, and they did it differently and I couldn't work out which way was better."

"Well I'm not *you*," said Miss Anderbel. "And neither are any of the other dancers you've seen. Everyone brings their own special style to each role. You need to dance as Natasha Marks, not as anyone else."

"I just thought…those other dancers are so much better than me. And I want to be like them when I grow up. I wish I could dance like them."

Tash could feel herself going bright red. She'd really thought that she was doing the right thing, trying her best to be as good as the ballerinas who had danced the Lilac Fairy before her. She wished this wasn't happening on the stage where everyone in the school could see and hear. She longed for a trapdoor to open up so that she could jump down it and disappear.

"You're just fine as you are," said Miss Anderbel firmly. "Or you were, before you started imitating other people. I told you when we gave you this role that it was because we knew that your personality and your own lovely style of dancing would bring something really special to the steps. Why would you bury that underneath copying other people? Be yourself, Tash! *That's* when you'll really be dancing your best."

"I'm sorry," said Tash. "I just wanted to be good."

"I understand," replied Miss Anderbel, and she smiled kindly at Tash. "When I was at school there were dancers who were my ballet idols and

I wanted to be exactly the same as them. But of course I wasn't, and couldn't ever be, for a million different reasons. It's no good trying to be other people. You need to be happy with who *you* are. If you can learn to do that, nothing can stop you."

Tash nodded. "I'll try," she said.

"*I* believe in you," said Miss Anderbel. "But that's not enough. *You* need to believe in you."

"Okay," said Tash.

She smiled at Miss Anderbel, wondering if this might be the most important ballet lesson she'd learned all year. She'd spent ages trying to dance like other people, when all along she should have been working on becoming the best dancer *she* could be.

She went back to her starting position, feeling as if the stage lights that shone down on everything had cleared away all the clouds of nervousness and worry. Standing in her tutu, she felt more like a ballerina than she ever had before. And as her body moved through the familiar steps, she felt more and more like herself, expressing the Lilac Fairy solo in her own way, her movements full of strength and grace and smiling friendliness.

She would never be anyone other than Tash Marks. But just as she would never be the same as anyone else, nobody else would ever be just like *her* either. That thought made her feel kind of powerful.

This was who she was: Tash the dancer, Tash the ballet-mad twelve year old, Tash the friend, who would find a way to bring Dani back to the love of ballet that she knew she still felt. She only had a day to do it, but she wouldn't give up.

Chapter 11

The night before the big end-of-year performance, Tash was so excited that she couldn't stop it escaping in giggles and bounces as she got ready for bed in Coppélia. She knew it was important to get a lot of rest so that she'd be able to dance better than ever the next day, so when Laura turned the light off she lay down, closed her eyes and tried really hard to fall asleep. But she couldn't.

It felt as if she lay awake for hours and hours,

but when she checked the time on her phone, hiding it under the covers so the light didn't wake anyone up, it wasn't even midnight yet. She listened to the familiar deep-sleep breathing of the others – all except Dani. Tiny gasps and jagged breaths were coming from Dani's bed. It sounded as if Dani was crying and trying really, really hard to keep silent.

"Dani?" Tash whispered.

Dani sniffed loudly but didn't say anything. Tash got out of bed and crept across to her friend. She sat on the side of Dani's bed and leaned down, giving her a hug. She felt Dani relax a bit and then she sat up.

"Sorry," Dani sniffed. "Did I wake you up?"

"No, I can't sleep. Do you want to talk?"

"Not here," Dani whispered.

She swung her legs over the side of the bed and fumbled for her slippers. Tash did the same and they shuffled out of the room and into the dark corridor.

There was a big window with a wide sill halfway down the stairs, and they settled themselves there, facing each other with their slippered feet touching in the middle. Dani stared out of the window at the dark shadows of trees on the school field.

"I'm going to tell Miss Anderbel I don't want to do the solo," she said without looking at Tash.

"What?" Tash gasped. "You *can't*, Dani!"

"I have to," said Dani. "I'm not going to get up on that stage and embarrass myself in front of everyone. It would be so horrible! Laura's my understudy, she could do it instead. She knows the solo as well as I do; she'll dance it much better than me."

"It's just nerves," said Tash. "Once you're onstage you'll be fine, I'm sure you will."

"You don't know that," said Dani. "I keep messing up in rehearsals when there's hardly anyone even watching. I'll be even worse when it's the real performance."

Tears started to slide down her cheeks.

"Dani…" Tash trailed off, not knowing what she could say to make her friend feel better.

She nudged Dani's foot with her own, wanting to show her somehow that her friends were there for her. Dani sniffed loudly, trying to stop crying.

Tash thought about how excited she was about her own performance. It felt wonderful and she loved it, and she wished she could give that feeling to Dani.

"What about your parents?" she asked. "They're coming to watch you dance! Don't you want them to see you on the City Ballet stage?"

"They're coming to watch Helen," Dani replied. "It won't matter at all if I'm dancing. I'll never, ever be as good at ballet as she is."

"Is that why you don't want to dance? Forget about Helen! Just dance for *you*."

"Easy for you to say," said Dani. "You don't have a sister."

"I have you," said Tash. "And Anisha. You're

like my sisters. And sisters look out for each other, and they don't let each other make big mistakes like this. *Please*, Dani. You *have* to dance."

Tash held Dani's eyes and silently begged her friend to trust her. But Dani only shook her head sadly.

"I can't," she whispered, and tears came again.

She slid down from the window sill and walked quickly away, brushing the tears from her face.

Tash had never seen Dani so sad before, not even after her fight with Helen. She was usually so cheerful and optimistic. The performance the next day was the most important ballet moment of the whole year – she couldn't let Dani miss out.

Back in Coppélia, Dani was hidden under her duvet, silent, but Tash guessed that she wasn't sleeping. She wanted to talk to Anisha, to tell her what Dani had said and try to come up with a way to make everything better, and she very nearly woke her up. But she looked at Anisha, deeply asleep with a small smile on her face, and she didn't want to disturb her. Whatever else happened, the rest of them still had to perform the next day.

With that thought in her mind, Tash climbed back into bed and tried to sleep, but every time she felt herself drifting off, sleep was pulled just out of reach by the memory of Dani's miserable face. By the time Tash eventually fell into slumber, she had worked herself up into desperate worry. She had to think of a brilliant idea to help Dani, and time was very nearly up.

No magic answer came to her in a dream, and the next morning, in snatched moments while Dani was in the bathroom, Tash told Anisha what had happened during the night.

"We have to stop her!" cried Anisha, horrified.

"But *how*?" asked Tash. Anisha looked back at her with helpless, sad eyes. She had no idea either.

* * *

When they arrived at the theatre that afternoon for the final dress rehearsal, Miss Anderbel was hurrying around busily with a clipboard and folders.

"I'm going to talk to her," said Dani.

"Dani…" began Tash, but Dani was already rushing after Miss Anderbel. Tash and Anisha followed her, desperately hoping that their teacher would tell Dani she had to dance.

"Miss Anderbel, I need to talk to you," said Dani, when they finally caught up with their teacher on the stairs leading up to their dressing room.

"Not now, girls," said Miss Anderbel. "I need to find Mr Watkins."

"But it's really, really important," said Dani.

Miss Anderbel sighed and finally looked up from her clipboard, giving Dani her full attention. Tash clenched her fingernails into the palms of her hands, dreading what Dani was going to say. And then Miss Anderbel's mobile phone rang and she answered it immediately.

"Sorry, Dani. Come and find me later, or see Miss Dixon if it's urgent. She's in charge of your year."

Miss Anderbel turned and hurried back down the stairs, talking into her phone, and Dani slumped against the wall.

"You might as well do the rehearsal," Tash said to Dani.

"Yeah, you can't just not be in the rehearsal without telling Miss Anderbel," said Anisha. "You'll get in huge trouble."

Tash nodded vigorously. Anisha was a genius!

"You're right," grumbled Dani. "Okay, I'll dance this afternoon, but as soon as the rehearsal's done I'm telling Miss Anderbel."

"Okay," agreed Tash. It wasn't okay at all, but she wasn't giving up yet. She had a whole afternoon now to convince Dani to dance in the performance, too. She just had to hope that the rehearsal didn't make things *worse*.

On the way back to their dressing room, they passed a rehearsal studio with big glass windows along one side. Tash stared at the City Ballet dancers using it and she recognized three of the soloists who'd come to talk to their class last term. She remembered how excited Dani had been to meet them then, and how they'd all talked about their dreams of dancing with City Ballet one day. She'd never have guessed that only a term later, Dani would be trying to drop out of the end-of-year show.

In the final rehearsal, Tash watched Dani's solo from the wings, just as she had done the day before. Dani was dancing better this time – much better! Tash was thrilled to see her get through the solo without forgetting any steps. She'd known all along that Dani could do it! Maybe she'd even change her mind about the performance now.

"That was great!" Tash whispered as Dani came offstage.

She held up her hand for a high five, but Dani only shrugged.

"Fluke," she said. "At least I don't ever have to do it again now."

"You mean you still want to pull out of the performance?" Tash asked. "But you can do it! You *just did*."

"Only because I thought it didn't matter any more," said Dani. "I can't do it in front of my parents and the teachers and a big massive audience. I know I'll mess it up and everyone will see that I'm just Helen's rubbish little sister."

"Dani, *no*," Tash insisted.

She couldn't say any more because Emma was walking gracefully off the stage and it was time for the Lilac Fairy solo. She ran out under the spotlights, but she was so worried about Dani that she couldn't smile. She hardly thought about her dancing at all, instead running through the steps mechanically. Luckily the Lilac Fairy steps were so embedded in her brain and her body that they were almost a part of her, and she could do them without thinking. Unluckily, thoughtless dancing was not what Miss Anderbel wanted to see.

"Tash, what is this?" cried her teacher during the group fairy dance. "More *sparkle*, please! Are you nervous about tonight? I know it's hard, but please try not to worry. Imagine that you're on the stage by yourself with no one watching. Just be yourself, and enjoy it!"

An idea hit Tash then, a plan so brilliant and risky that it almost knocked her *pirouette* off balance. She knew how to help Dani! She just had to make sure she got to her before Dani had a chance to talk to Miss Anderbel.

At the end of the dress rehearsal, Tash and her friends were standing in their finishing poses in neat lines, while Helen and Tom stood in the middle. Mr Watkins, Miss Anderbel and the other teachers clapped loudly.

"Well done, everyone," said Mr Watkins. "You've got three hours now to have a break before the performance. You can go out to the shops near the theatre if you like. Years Seven, Eight and Nine, school rules still apply so if you want to go out you need to have an older student or a teacher with you. If you are going out, you *must* be back here by six o'clock to get into costume and warm up."

The stage and auditorium was full of bustle as everyone chatted and decided what they were going to do.

"Let's stay here," Tash said immediately to Dani and Anisha.

"I'm going to talk to Miss Anderbel," said Dani.

"She's busy," said Tash, catching at Dani's arm and holding her back. "Let's change back into normal clothes first. Then we'll come and find her when there aren't so many people around."

Dani agreed and the three of them went back

to their dressing room. While Dani was in the toilet, Tash told Anisha her plan. Then she changed back into her clothes faster than she ever had before, and slipped out of the room to put the first stage of the plan into action.

When Tash returned to their dressing room, Dani was just pulling on her shoes. Anisha was already dressed and ready, sitting waiting on a chair. Tash gave her a little nod and then turned to Dani.

"We'll come with you to find Miss Anderbel," she said.

"Thanks," Dani replied. "I know you guys want me to perform, but I just can't do it. I'm sorry."

"We understand," said Anisha.

Tash glanced at her and they exchanged a look. They were taking a big risk. If the plan didn't work, there'd be no way of stopping Dani from going to Miss Anderbel. All would be lost. Tash took a deep breath.

"She's probably on the stage," she said.

But the stage was empty. Tash smiled: so far, so good.

"She's not here," said Dani. "She wouldn't have gone out. She must be around somewhere. Hey, where are you going?"

Tash and Anisha had walked out onto the silent stage, pulling their shoes and socks off as they went.

"Come back," Dani hissed at them from the wings.

Tash glanced out at the auditorium and saw Helen standing near the seats at the front. Tash gave her a questioning look and Helen grinned back and held up both thumbs, then moved towards the seats at the back so she couldn't be seen.

Tash tried to hold back a big grin as she beckoned to Dani, who shook her head and crossed her arms. Tash nodded and smiled at her but Dani still didn't move. Tash and Anisha went over to her and took one of her hands each, pulling her onto the stage with them.

The set was all ready for the first scene, *their* scene, with a beautiful backdrop painted shades of pale pink, blue and green, and with glittery gold thrones for the King and Queen on one side of the stage.

"We're not supposed to be here," said Dani.

"Come on," said Tash. "Let's dance."

"We've *already* danced," said Dani.

"But now it's just us," said Tash.

She started to spin and jump and twirl around the stage, making it up as she went along. She was doing this to help Dani, to get Dani to dance too, but it felt amazing and for a moment she forgot what she was here for. She was dancing on the City Ballet stage! Now that she wasn't worrying about the Lilac Fairy steps, she thought about all the famous feet that had danced on this stage before her, going back through years and years of treasured dancing history. She hoped that they might have left some of their talent on the stage and that it would shoot up through her feet and turn her into a City Ballet star too!

But then she remembered what Miss Anderbel had said, and she knew that she didn't need magical City Ballet talent to dance her best tonight. She just needed to believe in herself.

She spun out of one final turn and ended facing Dani.

"Miss Anderbel said something to me yesterday and I can't stop thinking about it," she said. "She told me that it's no good trying to be like other people. I can't compare myself to anyone else, because I'm *me*, so it'll never work. You have to stop comparing yourself, too, Dani. Forget about Helen, forget about every single dancer you've ever seen and just dance like you."

"Have fun!" added Anisha. "Dancing is the best thing ever, remember? We do it because we love it. So just...be on this stage right now, and dance, and love it."

"When you do that," continued Tash, "your dancing is happy and sunny and it's *amazing*."

"I wish I could get that back," whispered Dani.

She pointed her foot out in front of her and swept it around in a semicircular *ronde de jambe*. Her arms moved gracefully along with her leg, and then, as if she couldn't help herself, her head and her body were moving too and she began to dance across the stage, stopping to discard her shoes and socks and then dancing on.

Tash and Anisha watched her for a moment. She was smiling! And her chin was lifted so that she looked out towards the auditorium, full of grand rows of seats and little golden lights. Then Tash was dancing, too, and Anisha, and the three of them whirled through their steps from *The Sleeping Beauty* and added their own steps, leaps and turns, enjoying every second.

Tash felt more at home on the stage than she'd ever thought possible. It was only the second day she'd ever danced on it, but it already felt just as much hers as the studio at Aurora House.

Suddenly voices disturbed them. They froze

on the stage and stared at each other, and this time Tash wasn't able to stop a grin from lighting up her whole face.

"Should we hide?" Dani whispered, looking around desperately. "Why are you two grinning like that? What's going on?"

Before Tash or Anisha could answer, Dani's eyes went wide and her mouth fell open in awe. Three of the City Ballet dancers who had come to talk to their class at the beginning of last term walked onto the stage.

"I know we're not supposed to be here," Dani blurted out. "Sorry, we just wanted to dance and we couldn't stop ourselves."

She looked at Tash and Anisha and seemed confused that they weren't worried about being in trouble.

"Mind if we join in?" said Maria, one of the dancers.

Dani looked at Tash and Anisha again, and Tash couldn't help laughing as she shook her head to say she didn't mind. But she was too shy to come up with any words.

She was so glad that Helen was old enough to have been at Aurora House at the same time as Christine and Ruth, the other two dancers. It had been Tash's idea to ask them to come and dance on the stage with Dani, Anisha and herself. But she would never have been brave enough to ask them! That was where Helen had come in. Tash had guessed that if Helen knew how upset Dani was, she'd want to help, and she'd been right.

The ballerinas still had their pointe shoes on from their practice session, and they started to dance. Tash watched open-mouthed as Maria spun across the stage, but then Maria started to do the Lilac Fairy steps. Tash joined in, smiling and laughing and knowing that she'd wake up tomorrow, unable to believe that she'd danced onstage with a dancer from her favourite ballet company.

Her friends were dancing now, too – Anisha

whirled around the stage with Ruth, both of them making steps up as they went along, and Dani had started to dance her solo again. Then Christine started to do the steps of Dani's solo along with her.

To begin with, Dani was so absorbed in the dance that she didn't even notice, but then she turned and saw graceful Christine performing the same steps perfectly beside her. Tash noticed a look of alarm flash into Dani's eyes, and she worried that Dani would get nervous and forget the steps again, but Dani didn't stop dancing for one moment. All her fear seemed to slide away from her into the darkness of the wings. Happiness shone out from her fingertips to her pointed toes.

They danced around the stage together and Tash saw Dani exchange an excited grin with Christine as their feet flitted through the pretty steps. Dani was dancing better than ever, and no one needed to remind her to keep her eyes up or to smile, because she couldn't stop herself. Tash thought that she looked so confident that she might float up to the bright stage lights above them.

"I love those steps," Christine said when they'd finished the solo.

"Me too," agreed Dani.

They smiled at each other again, then Dani danced over to Tash and Anisha.

"That was amazing!" she squealed and they laughed too.

"Good luck for this evening," said Maria.

"We'll be in the audience, so we'll look out for you!" said Christine.

"Thanks," Tash, Dani and Anisha managed to say in the middle of gasps and giggles and excited hopping.

When the dancers had gone, Tash heard someone else walking onto the stage. They all turned and saw Helen coming towards them.

"That was so much fun to watch," she said.

Tash looked anxiously at Dani, who was staring at Helen, her face caught halfway between the big smile that had been there before and a look of shock at finding out her sister had been there the whole time.

"You were brilliant, Dani."

"You were watching?" said Dani.

"You're going to dance so beautifully tonight," said Helen.

"Do you really think so?" Dani asked.

Helen nodded. "You'll be a perfect fairy, I just know it. My friends are sick of me going on about how my little sister's only in Year Seven and already has a solo! I'm really proud of you."

Dani looked as if she couldn't believe what she was hearing, but she managed to stammer a thanks.

"I'm proud of you too," she said.

"I hope I don't let everyone down," said Helen.

"Of course you won't!" gasped Dani. "You'll be brilliant. Everyone knows how good you are."

"That just makes me more worried! I've been given this amazing chance, to dance the main role in the ballet, and if I'm not as good as people expect me to be, then they'll be disappointed."

"You have to not think about that," Dani told her. "Just dance for yourself."

She smiled at Tash, and Tash nodded. She was so glad that she'd been able to help Dani feel more confident.

"I'm sorry I've been so horrible to you this term," said Dani.

"I'm sorry too," said Helen. "I should have noticed that you were worrying and tried to help sooner. I didn't realize until Tash told me you wanted to pull out of the performance, and that she had a plan to get the City Ballet dancers to help you remember how much you love ballet."

"You guys did all that for me?" Dani gasped.

"That's how much we want you to dance tonight," said Helen.

"Thank you!" said Dani, and grabbed Helen into a hug. Then she turned to Tash and Anisha and hugged them too. "You're the most amazing friends in the world."

"We had to make you remember that dancing's fun when you're not worrying about being as good as someone else," said Tash.

"You did a good job," said Dani. "Because that was the most fun thing ever."

"I'm not so sure," said Tash with a smile. "I think the most fun thing *ever* is going to be the performance tonight."

Dani bit her lip, still a little nervous, but then she shook it off and her happy Dani smile shone through.

"You know what?" she said. "I think you're right."

Chapter 12

"Here we are!" said Tash.

She spread the programme out flat on the skirt of her tutu so that the others could see it too. She and Dani were sitting on the counter underneath the mirrors in the Year Thirteen dressing room. Helen was sitting in front of the mirror doing her make-up for the performance, and Anisha was excitedly dancing about in front of Tash and Dani, dressed in the purple tutu with silver sparkles that all the Lilac Fairy attendants would be wearing. Her black hair was pulled up into a bun and her head was crowned with a wreath of little purple flowers, held in place by half a packet of hairpins.

Years Seven and Eight had had their make-up done for them because they hadn't learned to do stage make-up properly yet, and now, dressed in their tutus with their Aurora House zip-up hoodies on over the top to keep warm, they looked more like ballerinas than ever.

Anisha stopped dancing to look at where Tash was pointing at the glossy programme. There was a page for each scene of the ballet and all their names were listed next to their roles. Tash looked at the very first one:

Lilac Fairy....................... Natasha Marks

She felt a nervous thrill fluttering in her stomach and it made her tense all her muscles. There was her own name in a proper ballet programme! All the parents who had come to see the older students would see it, and when she stepped onto the stage in her Lilac Fairy costume, they'd know who she was. It was exciting, but she felt the pressure of it, too. She was going to be representing Aurora House. She really wanted to do well and make the school proud.

She looked further down the list and saw Danielle Taylor listed as the first fairy, and Anisha Acharya as the first of the Lilac Fairy attendants. Dani was looking at it, too, over her shoulder, and Anisha leaned in to see.

"Mum and Dad texted me to say good luck," Dani said to Helen, when she could see that her sister had finished her make-up.

Helen reached for her phone and looked at the screen.

"Me too," she said.

She fiddled with the phone for a moment then she paused and looked over her shoulder. There was no one else in the room at the moment. "Can you guys keep a secret?"

They all nodded eagerly and leaned in. Tash gripped the edge of the counter with her fingertips to stop herself sliding off.

"Mr Watkins just told me that the City Ballet Company is going to offer me a position in their *corps de ballet*!"

Tash's hands flew to her mouth in shock, then she remembered her make-up and took them down again.

"That's amazing!" she gasped.

"Wow," said Anisha.

Dani still hadn't said anything, but she was looking at her sister with a big smile and the same look of awe she'd had when Helen had told them she was going to be Aurora in the show. She jumped down from the counter to give Helen a hug. Tash watched them become a smiling, laughing tangle of tutus and she knew that everything between Dani and her sister was okay again.

"I'm so happy for you!" said Dani. "Tell me the second I'm allowed to start showing off about it."

Helen laughed, then the door opened and some of the other Year Thirteen students came in.

"You guys are on soon," one of them said to Tash and the others.

"Yeah, we should go," said Anisha.

They headed for the door.

"Good luck," said Helen.

They all turned and smiled at her. Tash was thinking that one day soon she would come to this theatre to watch City Ballet perform and Helen would be onstage, someone she'd been at school with! Somehow the dream that one day Tash might get to be in the company herself felt even closer.

Dani ran back over to Helen and gave her another hug, crushing their tutu skirts together, her pale yellow and green against Helen's light pink.

"I love you," she said quietly.

"I love you too." Helen hugged Dani tightly for another moment, then pushed her away. "Now go and dance."

Sparkling Solo

* * *

Tash stood in the wings watching the Year Eights dancing onstage. The music was building up to her entrance, and the nerves inside her were building too. Dani was a few people ahead of her, nearer to the stage, and Anisha was right behind her. Dani slipped back in the final minute before they had to go on.

"Good luck," she whispered, and she gave Tash's hand a squeeze.

Tash reached behind her for Anisha's hand.

"Good luck," she whispered over her shoulder to Anisha.

"Have fun," Anisha reminded them both.

Tash nodded and gave Anisha a huge smile. Even in the darkness of the wings, she could see Anisha's eyes sparkling happily back at her as Dani hurried to her place at the front of the line of fairies. And then they were on.

Dani led them all out onto the stage, running on *demi-pointe* to the twinkling music. Tash forced her face into a big, happy Lilac Fairy smile, even though inside she was so nervous she was starting to feel sick.

The stage was bright and the auditorium was so dark that she couldn't see any faces. She knew Mum was out there somewhere, and so were Miss Anderbel and Mr Watkins and old Ms Hartley, the school's founder. Not to mention the hundreds of parents and friends and relatives who were there to watch the other students but who would still notice if Tash messed anything up.

"I'm dancing for me, I'm being myself," she repeated silently to herself, and soon her smile became real.

The music was beautiful and her lovely lilac-coloured tutu shone with colour and glitter under the stage lights. With every step, she felt the nerves and excitement lifting her higher than she'd been able to jump in rehearsals, spinning her round faster and more neatly in her turns and helping her to glide across the stage as if she was skimming across clouds. She could see that Dani was having a great time, too, and it was infectious; the more she saw her friends smile, the more she smiled herself.

Theatres had always felt like special places to Tash. She loved doing ballet classes and the rehearsals had been fun, but nothing in the world compared to what it felt like to dance onstage with an audience watching every step, especially when you were dancing with your best friends. No matter what happened after tonight, they would always have this special moment, shared by the three of them, held together by the magic of the theatre.

At the end of the fairy group dance, Tash followed the others offstage, walking gracefully the way they'd been taught. As soon as she was in the wings, she dropped her arms and gulped water down from the bottle she'd left on the table. Dani's solo was next. Tash found a space in the wings to watch, and wrapped her arms around her stomach.

Dani walked onto the stage with her head held high and stood ready to begin. The music started and she began to glide smoothly through the steps. Tash ticked the sections off in her mind. So far, no mistakes. Even better, Dani was smiling! Her eyes were up and she was looking out towards the audience, shining with happiness. She was good!

She finished triumphantly and the audience burst into loud applause. Tash clapped quietly along with them from the wings, bouncing on the balls of her feet in excitement. She couldn't wait to give Dani a hug and tell her how brilliant she was. Dani finished her curtsey and walked off the stage.

"Well done, well done, you were so good!" Tash whispered as she grabbed her.

Dani's hands were shaking.

"That felt amazing," Dani whispered. "You're going to enjoy your solo *so* much!"

"No talking," whispered a teacher behind them, and Tash and Dani both pressed their lips closed.

Anisha came up behind them and hugged Dani. They all looked at each other, full of all the happy things they wanted to say, but not able to speak. Their eyes spoke for them, full of joy, and their hands mimed clapping without making any noise.

Soon it was Tash's turn, and a mixture of excitement and dread about her own solo and pure happiness for Dani made her heartbeat fast and light. Her arms and legs and feet couldn't keep still, she was so desperate to get out there and *dance*. But as soon as the music started and she was moving through the steps, her nerves settled and she was able to enjoy it.

She felt her body move through the same steps she'd danced every day for weeks; they were familiar but they felt different tonight, bigger and grander and full of magic, even though she knew that she was only pretending to be a fairy. This minute, this moment, this was the most special thing she'd ever felt.

As she finished, listened to the audience clapping, and curtseyed, she hoped that Mum and the rest of the audience had been able to feel a piece of the magic, too.

Year Seven and Eight all had to go back to their dressing rooms after their scene, so they didn't get to watch Helen doing her big, difficult solo in the second scene, or the Year Eleven and Twelve scene after the short interval. Instead, they played card games, tried to eat cereal bars without messing up their lipstick, sang and shouted and laughed and let out all their excited energy in as many ways as they could without getting told off by Miss Dixon, who was in charge of their dressing room.

"Where's my flower wreath?" wailed Donna when it was time to go down to the stage for the final scene. "I'm sure I left it here!"

She was lifting hoodies and leg warmers and books up, looking under them and then dropping them to the floor.

Sparkling Solo

"I don't know how you lot have managed to make such a mess in only one day," tutted Miss Dixon. "You're going to have to clear it all up before you go tonight."

"But I need my wreath now," said Donna. "I can't be the only Lilac Fairy attendant without one!"

"We've got to go," said Anisha. "We're on in five minutes."

"I can't go without it," cried Donna.

"You'll have to," said Miss Dixon. "Is everyone here?" she started to do a headcount as the girls gathered by the door.

"Dani, take your leg warmers off!" said Tash with a giggle.

Dani gasped and looked down at her legs, which were covered by very un-fairy-like black leg-warmers with silvery sparkly threads running through them. She pulled them off and threw them towards her own messy corner of the room.

"Ready?" asked Miss Dixon. "Come on, Donna, you're out of time."

Donna stared glumly at her reflection in the mirror and then joined the group by the door.

Miss Dixon led them down the stairs and through the grey corridors. They reached the heavy door to the stage where they had to wait in silence. It felt as if they were standing there for ages, but then the door opened and the Year Eleven and Twelve students streamed out. Tash watched them pass, completely in awe of their grace as they walked up the stairs. Then Miss Dixon led them into the wings.

While she was waiting to go on, Tash felt someone tap her shoulder and turned around.

"Pass this to Donna," whispered Lily-May, handing Tash a flower wreath. "I found it on the table over there. Donna must have put it down and forgotten."

Tash passed it forward to Toril, who passed it on to Anisha, and it made its way down the line to Donna. Tash knew when it had reached her because there was a quick gasp and a squeaked thanks, and then the sound of Miss Dixon telling her to be quiet.

Then the stage was set for the last scene and the curtain rose on the two Year Thirteens who were playing the King and Queen in the final scene. When their music came on, Tash and her friends ran out onto the stage one last time.

For most of the scene they just had to stand around looking fairy-like, which was more difficult than it sounded, because they had to keep smiling the whole time. Tash's face ached from it, but she was really enjoying watching all the older students dance, all of them giving everything they had for their last-ever performance as Aurora House dancers.

By the time Helen and Tom took up their places for their final *pas de deux*, Tash was starting to feel that it was impossible to smile for a second longer. But Helen and Tom lit up the stage with their steps, and she couldn't help grinning every time she saw them do something that she knew was really difficult or something they'd had trouble with in rehearsals. They were completely perfect tonight.

Tash turned her head slightly to look at Dani and Anisha, who were standing next to her in the line. Dani was watching Helen with shining eyes. She looked almost as happy now as she had when she was dancing her own solo earlier.

Finally it was time for the big group dance, and as Tash jumped and skipped and stepped across the stage in time with her classmates and the older students, she felt her heart swelling with pride and love. The music changed, became grander and louder, and as it started to build up towards the end of the ballet, the students from all the other years rushed onto the stage in neat lines.

Tash's year danced forward so that by the last note of the music, Year Seven were lined up across the front of the stage, with Year Eight behind them, and then all the other years in order of age. They left an aisle down the middle and Helen and

Tom finished centre stage, as applause and cheers rang out from the audience.

Tash was so happy she almost laughed. She exchanged a grin with Dani and Anisha as they curtseyed. Then Year Seven and Eight ran off into the wings so that Year Nine and Ten could step forward and be applauded.

Silence in the wings didn't matter any more and everyone was talking and hugging each other and jumping around excitedly. It had been a long, exhausting day and Tash knew that she'd be tired eventually, but right now, she felt as if she could go back onstage and dance the whole thing again.

"I still can't believe that was *you* up there, my little Tash dancing onstage, as brilliant as any ballerina."

"*Mum*," said Tash with a laugh.

"You were *wonderful*," insisted Mum.

She hugged Tash again, trying not to damage the lovely flowers she'd just given her. The theatre lobby was a noisy crush of dancers and parents and teachers. Tash had already been hugged by Mum at least ten times, and had been told how fantastic she was twenty times or more.

It seemed like months ago that Dani had told her she didn't want to be in the show – was it possible that it had only been last night? So much had happened since then.

A couple of metres away, Dani was hugging her own mum while Helen hugged their dad. They were each holding flowers too. Their parents had bought them both the same flowers, and were hugging Dani just as much as Helen and telling her all the same lovely things they were saying to her sister. Someone passing by would never have been able to tell that Helen was the star of the show.

"You were brilliant," Dani's mum said to Tash.

"Thanks," said Tash. "So was Dani."

She shared a smile with Dani.

Anisha dragged her parents over then, and the adults got talking, so the three of them slipped away to the side.

"Look!" said Anisha. "My dad took this photo at the end of the performance." She showed Tash and Dani a picture on her dad's mobile phone. Tash looked at herself, standing elegantly in her pretty tutu with a happy smile on her face. She knew that she was still smiling just as much now, and when she looked at her friends, she saw the same love of ballet and joy at performing written on their faces too.

All three of them still had their hair up in ballet buns, stiff with hairspray, and their eyes were outlined with stage make-up and sprinkles of glitter. Even now that they were dressed back in jeans and their school hoodies, they looked completely like dancers. Tash didn't want to brush the hairspray out of her hair or wipe the make-up from her face – that would mean the show was over, and she wasn't ready for that yet.

"We get to do this every summer for six more years," she said, reminding herself that this wasn't just a once-in-a-lifetime chance.

"I know!" said Dani. "I can't wait!"

Tash smiled at her. It was amazing how much more confident and happy Dani was now that she wasn't comparing herself to Helen any more.

Tash thought about how she'd spent the whole term comparing herself to other dancers, too, and she promised herself that she'd never do that again. Next year, when it came to the big performance, she was going to spend the whole term just dancing as herself, and it was going to feel as wonderful as this day had, all over again.

But for now, she only wanted to enjoy the theatre magic that still filled her heart. After the long drive tonight, tomorrow morning she'd wake up at home with Mum and it would be the summer holidays. A long stretch without ballet classes waited for her, and beyond that, a new year full of ballet steps to learn. But tonight she was the Lilac Fairy, and she wanted to hold on to that for as long as possible.

"We'd better go back to school to pick up your

things, Tash," said Mum. "We need to get going if we're going to be home before midnight."

"Yes, us too," said Anisha's mum.

Dani's family lived too far away to go home tonight, so they were staying in a hotel near the theatre and would travel home the next day. Tash hugged Dani tightly.

"Well done," Tash said. "You were amazing today."

"You were the amazing one," said Dani. "Thank you for making me dance. I can't believe I almost missed out on this."

"I'd never have let that happen," said Tash.

They hugged each other again. Anisha hugged Dani too, and then she and Tash and their families went out into the night. Tash held her flowers close to her chest and ducked her head down to smell them. They were lilac coloured and perfect, just like the whole evening had been.

As she walked down the road to Mum's car, Tash looked back over her shoulder at the theatre.

One day she'd be grown up, and maybe she'd still be walking out of theatres after performances with beautiful flowers in her arms. But even if she was, she didn't know if any ballet performance would ever feel as special as this one.

Basic Ballet Positions

All of the wonderful ballet moves Tash, Dani and Anisha learn begin and end in one of these five basic positions...

First position
The feet point in opposite directions, with heels touching. Arms are rounded to the front.

Second position
The feet point in opposite directions, with heels spaced approximately thirty centimetres apart. Arms are out to the sides, angled down and forward.

Third position

One foot is placed in front
of the other so that the heel
of the front foot is near the arch
of the back foot. One arm is in
first position, the other is in
second position.

Fourth position

One foot is placed approximately
thirty centimetres in front of the
other. One arm is rounded
and raised above the head,
the other is in second position.

Fifth position

One foot is placed in front of the
other, with the heel of one foot in
contact with the toe of the other
foot. Both arms are rounded
and raised above the head.

Ballet Glossary

adage The name for the slow steps in the centre of the room, away from the barre.

arabesque A beautiful balance on one leg.

assemblé A jump where the feet come together at the end.

attitude A pose standing on one leg, the other leg raised with the knee bent.

battement glisse A faster version of *battement tendu*, with the foot lifted off the floor.

battement tendu A foot exercise where you stretch one leg out along the floor, keeping it straight all the way to the point of the foot.

chassé A soft smooth slide of the feet.

demi-pointe Dancing with the weight of the body on the toes and the ball of the foot.

développé A lifting and unfolding of one leg into the air, while balancing on the other.

en pointe Dancing on the very tips of the toes.

entrechat A jump directly upward, while crossing the feet before and behind several times in the air.

grand battement A high kick, keeping the supporting leg straight.

jeté A spring where you land on the opposite foot.

pas de bourrée Tiny little steps to the side, like a mouse.

pas de chat A cat hop from one foot to the other.

plié The first step practised in each class. You have to bend your knees slowly and make sure your feet are turned right out, with your heels firmly planted on the floor for as long as possible.

port de bras Arm movements.

révérence The curtsey at the end of class.

rond de jambe This is where you make a circle with your leg.

sissonne en arrière A jump from two feet onto one foot moving backwards.

sissonne en avant A jump from two feet onto one foot moving forwards.

soubresaut A jump off two feet, pointing your feet hard in the air.

turnout You have to stand with your legs and feet and hips all opened out and pointing to the side, not the front. This is the most important thing in ballet that everyone learns right from the start.

Usborne Quicklinks

For links to websites where you can watch
videos of ballet dancers, see excerpts of ballet
performances and find out more about ballet,
go to the Usborne Quicklinks Website at
www.usborne-quicklinks.com and enter
the keywords "ballet stars".

When using the Internet, make sure you follow the Internet safety
guidelines displayed on the Usborne Quicklinks Website. Usborne
Publishing is not responsible for the content on any website other
than its own. We recommend that children are supervised while
on the Internet, that they do not use Internet chat rooms, and that
you use Internet filtering software to block unsuitable material.
For more information, see the "Net Help" area on the Usborne
Quicklinks Website.

Usborne Publishing is not responsible and does not accept liability
for the availability or content of any website other than its own,
or for any exposure to harmful, offensive, or inaccurate material
which may appear on the Web. Usborne Publishing will have no
liability for any damage or loss caused by viruses that may be
downloaded as a result of browsing the sites it recommends.

Follow all of Tash's
Ballet Star dreams
in two other
sparkling stories...

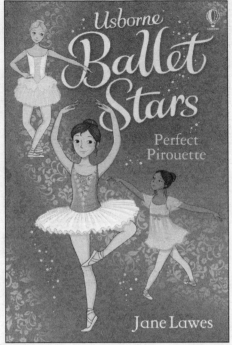

❊ Perfect Pirouette ❊

It's Tash's first term at Aurora House, and she's thrilled
to be living with other girls who love ballet just as much
as she does! But when she starts to worry that her
dancing isn't as good as her new friends', Tash decides
to take a big risk. Will her plan lead to a perfect
pirouette...or a dancing disaster?

ISBN 9781409583530

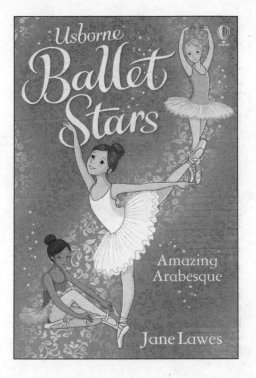

✿ Amazing Arabesque ✿

It's Tash's second term at Aurora House, and she's thrilled to be back – especially when she realizes she'll be learning to dance *en pointe*! But when Anisha starts acting strangely in class, Tash is worried. Their first ballet exam is coming up, and Anisha isn't even *trying* to master the tricky *arabesque*. Can Tash get her back on track before it's too late?

ISBN 9781409583547

Also by Jane Lawes

ISBN: 9781409531791

Summertime and Somersaults

Tara loves gym and spends all her time practising in her garden. When she joins Silverdale Gym Club she's catapulted into their star squad. But there's so much to learn. How will she ever catch up with her talented teammates?

Friendships and Backflips

Tara's training for her first ever competition and she's desperate to win a gold medal. But she's so busy learning the tricky routine that her best friends think she's deserted them. Can she find room in her life for her friends *and* gym?

ISBN: 9781409531807

Handsprings and Homework

Tara's through to a national competition, but she's training so hard that her homework is starting to pile up and she's in big trouble with her teachers. Can Tara finish all her work on time *and* win a gold medal?

ISBN: 9781409531814

For more *dazzling* reads
head to
www.usborne.com/fiction